BROKEN SILENCE

#15 OF THE

'Hawkman Series'

by

Betty Sullivan La Pierre

Others in 'The Hawkman Series'
by
BETTY SULLIVAN LA PIERRE
www.bettysullivanlapierre.com

THE ENEMY STALKS
DOUBLE TROUBLE
THE SILENT SCREAM
DIRTY DIAMONDS
BLACKOUT
DIAMONDS aren't FOREVER
CAUSE FOR MURDER
ANGELS IN DISGUISE
IN FOR THE KILL
GRAVE WEB
THE LURE OF THE WITCH
SHADOWS IN THE NIGHT
THE ARCHER
MOONSHINE MURDER

Also by Betty Sullivan La Pierre

MURDER.COM
THE DEADLY THORN

This novel is a work of fiction. The characters, names, incidents, dialogue, and plot are the products of the author's imagination or used fictitiously. Any resemblance to actual person, companies, or events is purely coincidental.

I want to dedicate this book to
Selma Rubler
and
Anne Pina

"BROKEN SILENCE"

#15 'Hawkman Series'

CHAPTER ONE

Saturday morning, Hawkman had promised his wife, Jennifer, he'd take her to see the eagle nests. She'd been watching the birth and growth of a family of Bald Eagles on her computer. They had intrigued her to such a point, she wanted to check out the ones on Copco Lake. The power company had made platforms on top of their high lines to accommodate the raptors in the area. Jennifer had seen the ospreys, but the eagles had nested farther north.

They climbed into the 4X4, Jennifer with her camera hanging off her shoulder and binoculars around her neck. "I hope they're still in the fledging phase and haven't completely left the nest."

Hawkman glanced at her. "They still depend on the parents to bring them food, so they return to the nest for several weeks while the adults are teaching them to hunt and fly."

She smiled. "I hope they're still at that stage."

"They're just big black birds with raptor features and large wings until they mature."

Jennifer nodded. "They're so fascinating. I can see why you loved the study of ornithology."

"Strange as it may seem, the eagle is lazy and doesn't expend any more energy than necessary. They teach their young to steal food from other birds, and how to spot road kill. They nest near streams, since fish is their favorite food."

She grinned. "I have to say the father eagle is an expert in defurring and defeathering the prey. I had a good laugh when the nest was suddenly filled with raccoon fur and then the wind whipped it away."

Hawkman pointed toward the top of a big high-line tower with a gigantic array of sticks around the edge of the man-built platform. "I'm pretty sure that's an eagle's nest. There's another up the road. We"ll check this one, and if we don't see any action, I'll drive to the next one."

She rolled down the window and put the binoculars to her eyes. "Don't get too close. I don't want to spook them."

He stopped several yards away, and took out the glasses he always carried in the glove compartment. They both studied the nest for several minutes.

Jennifer climbed out of the vehicle and quietly closed the door. "I'm not sure there's anything going on in this nest. I'm going to venture closer and see if I notice any evidence they've been here."

"Look for white poop around the perimeter."

She gave him a thumbs up as she made her way toward the tower. Just as she disappeared behind some high weeds and brush, Hawkman heard a loud scream. He bounded out of the 4X4 and sprinted toward the area where she'd vanished.

Jumping over the tall bushes he almost stumbled over her crouched figure. She put a finger to her lips. He knelt beside her.

"Are you okay?"

"Yes," she whispered. Did you hear that scream?"

"I thought it was you," he said. "It sure sounded like someone in distress. Any idea where it came from."

She pointed in front of her.

About that time, something walking through the thicket made them jerk toward the noise. They both laughed when several peacocks strutted into the small clearing under the tall tower.

Hawkman raised up, causing the birds to scurry back into the underbrush. "Never thought of those noisy critters being around here. When they scream, it sounds like a woman who needs help."

Jennifer shook her head, stood and stared at the top of the tower. She studied the area directly under the huge nest. "I see no evidence there have been eaglets raised here. Let's drive to the next one."

They trooped back to the 4X4 and headed up the dirt road approximately a half mile. Jennifer immediately grabbed her binoculars when they spotted the large round structure on top of another tower.

"There's definitely something going on here," she said, scooting to the edge of the seat. "Stop."

Hawkman found a place to pull the vehicle off to the side without blocking the road. He put his binoculars to his face. "Oh, yeah. I can see two black eaglets. They're waiting for food from mom or dad."

She continued to watch, grinning. "Wish I could see down on the nest, instead of having to look up at it."

"I wouldn't advise you to move too close or you're liable to come home painted in white poop. Those young 'uns aim for it to go over the railing and don't care what's underneath as long as it clears their home."

"Understood, but I think I can make it a little closer without getting hit." She slid out of the 4X4, her glasses dangling around her neck and camera in hand.

Hawkman smiled as he watched her head into the brush. He decided to follow and quietly climbed out of the vehicle. Soon they both stood below the nest. Jennifer had caught a beautiful picture of the adult flying in with a squirrel clutched in its talons. The squealing of the eaglets carried through the air as they attacked their meal with vigor.

"Wonder which one covered or mantled it?" Jennifer asked.

Hawkman chuckled. "If they haven't learned how to defur, the one who grabbed it might give it up until it's cleaned enough to eat, then try stealing it again."

"They are sly," Jennifer said, staring up. Then she pointed as the adult left. "Looks like mom or dad are leaving it up to the babies."

"The parents will watch at a distance, and return to help if the eaglets aren't successful."

"I think I've seen enough. Thanks for bringing me out here. It makes my day to think we have nesting eagles in our area."

"These parents will more than likely nest here again next year. It's also possible the youngsters will return in four or five years after they've sown their wild oats," Hawkman said, taking her arm as they climbed down a small incline toward the road. Just as they reached the 4X4, a loud scream echoed through the trees.

Hawkman pushed Jennifer into the passenger side and slammed the door. "Stay down. That was no peacock."

Running back toward the tall tower, he pulled his Beretta from his shoulder holster. Crouching, he surveyed the area, but saw nothing suspicious. After a few minutes of staying hidden, he moved to a small knoll and searched the surroundings farther out with his binoculars. A thin curl of smoke circling above the tree tops caught his attention.

CHAPTER TWO

Jennifer crunched low in the seat of the 4X4 until she couldn't stand the suspense, and cautiously raised her head. She didn't see Hawkman anywhere. The window on the passenger side remained rolled down, but she didn't dare call out to him.

"Darn, why didn't I bring my gun", she mumbled.

She'd heard the scream clearly and would have sworn someone yelled, "Run, baby run." Jennifer wondered if the other shriek really came from the peacocks. Sound travels a long way when there are no obstructions.

Her curiosity had just about gotten the best of her, when Hawkman emerged jogging out of the forest. Binoculars bouncing off his chest and gun in hand, he jumped into the driver's side.

"Did you find who cried out?"she asked.

He holstered his weapon, righted his hat, and shook his head. "No, I saw nothing suspicious. However, there is a house or cabin down in the valley. I'm not sure how to get to it, but I have a map at home of this area. I could see a path which looked like an overgrown dirt road. Maybe the map will show a way to get to it."

"I'm not sure I heard right, but it sounded like someone was urging a child to run. Is that what you heard?" Jennifer asked.

Hawkman maneuvered the 4X4 until he'd turned it around and soon headed back the way they'd come. "Yeah, but I didn't see any signs of a person, or even a building. Only a thin column of smoke curling above the trees which looked like it came from a chimney."

"You sure it wasn't a fire starting?"

"Yes. I watched for a while, and it didn't grow."

She made a face. "Who in the world would live way out here in the boonies?"

He shrugged. "Could be a mountain man who built a log cabin."

"Guess so, and he found a mountain woman; then they had a mountain kid whom she told to 'run baby run'." She muffled a giggle behind her hand. "Sorry, that was a mean comment."

He grinned. "You could be right and they might have just been playing a mountain game with their offspring. It could all be very harmless."

Jennifer frowned. "The tone of voice I heard didn't appear playful; it sounded very serious, like scared."

"There's a very thin line in what you hear between excitement of a game and a frightful cry."

She thought a moment. "You're probably right. It would be hard to distinguish one from the other unless you were there in person."

"Once I find a way to get to that sector, my best bet would be to observe it first, before I came to any conclusion."

They soon drove into their own driveway and went inside. Hawkman immediately went back to his office and brought out the county map he'd picked up a year or so ago. Jennifer went to her computer and plugged in her camera to check the pictures she'd taken of the eagles.

Flattening the large map out on the dining room table, Hawkman sat down and began to trace where they'd been. He marked with a pencil the raptor's nest location and checked the outlying territory. Furrowing his brow, he studied where he thought he'd seen the smoke, but found no evidence of a building or road. However, there were marked trails which led to and around the area. Someone could easily drive on them as the land appeared relatively flat. Scratching his sideburn, he glanced over at Jennifer. "Did the pictures turn out?"

"Yes, especially the one of the parent eagle bringing in the prey."

He got up and stood behind her to view the photos. "Excellent. You caught not only the color, but the large wing spread, which shows the size of the raptor."

She looked up at him. "How's your search going?"

"Puzzling. This map is not old, yet I don't find any sign of a structure where I thought I saw smoke, nor a road, only trails."

"Is it possible someone was just camping?"

"Yes, there's a chance I misjudged the gray stream coming through the trees."

"Did you find an easy way to get to the area?" Jennifer said, rising from her chair and moving toward the map.

Hawkman ran his finger along the route they'd taken to see the eagle nests. "We could continue along this road, though I'm not sure how rough it might be. I doubt it's been used much past the site of the nests." He continued tracing with the erasure end of a pencil. "It would take us down the hill where we'd have to make a sharp turn to the left and hunt for one of these trails. Or we could veer off to the left on that fork in the road before heading up the hill to the high line towers."

She tapped her chin with her finger. "Unfortunately, that road takes off on a tangent, far from where you want to go."

"I'm thinking about taking the Polaris four-wheeler. It could manage the hills and gorges much easier than the SUV."

She nodded. "You realize I'm going with you."

"There's no need, and it could be dangerous."

"I'll be there to protect your back. Never again will I leave this house to go up into the hills without my gun. I don't like being vulnerable."

"If you insist; but first, let's grab a sandwich, then get on the road while we have plenty of daylight left."

Hawkman went into the garage and quickly serviced the Polaris while Jennifer fixed sandwiches, grabbed her fanny pack containing her gun, shoved extra clips inside, then fastened it around her waist and slapped a ball cap over her short curly locks.

After they downed their meals, they each grabbed a couple of bottled waters and put them into the saddle bags on the four-wheeler. Soon they were on the road heading toward the eagle's nest.

Once they reached the tower, the hill crested and Hawkman had to gear down as they traveled the sharp incline. He discovered his assumption that little traffic had ensued past the nest appeared to be correct. High weeds covered the center of the road and the tire tracks on each side were slowly being covered with vegetation.

He stopped the Polaris and removed a piece of paper from his jeans jacket pocket, where he'd sketched a map.

"Is there a problem?" Jennifer asked, looking over his shoulder.

"I'm hoping these paths leading to the area are not so overgrown we can't recognize them. Thought I'd check the distance from where we came down, to where the trail intersects with this road." He waved a hand. "Keep an eye out for about the next twenty yards and let me know if you see anything resembling such."

He moved ahead slowly as both watched the side of the road, studying the landscape.

Suddenly, Jennifer poked him on the shoulder.

Hawkman brought the four-wheeler to a halt. "You see something?"

"Yes, but it's not a trail. It looks like a dog."

"A dog?"

She pointed behind the Polaris. "He's following us. He's in the tall weeds and I just got a glimpse of him."

Hawkman twisted around in his seat and examined the swaying plants. "I see him. What's he doing in this godforsaken place?"

"He must belong to the people we think are here."

He turned off the four-wheeler. "Let's just sit here for a while and see what he does."

Five minutes passed before the animal poked his head out of the brush and whined. He then barked and headed back into the thicket. When Hawkman or Jennifer didn't move, he came back and repeated the action.

Hawkman rubbed his chin. "I think he wants us to follow him."

"Same feeling I have. Shall we?"

Hawkman nodded and climbed off the Polaris, then helped Jennifer disembark.

CHAPTER THREE

Hawkman took Jennifer's hand as they stepped into the brush behind the dog. Only then did they get a good look at the mix of a Golden Labrador retriever.

"He's a beautiful animal," Hawkman commented, in a low voice.

"It's a she," Jennifer said.

The animal bounded ahead at a pace they couldn't keep up with, but the dog would circle and come back for them, barking as she led them deeper into the forest.

"I sure hope we don't get lost," Jennifer said.

"We won't. If you'll notice, we're on a trail. Probably the one on the map, but the weeds have grown up at the entry onto the road; that's why we didn't spot it."

They hadn't gone far before the dog stopped at a fallen log, looked down and whined. A hand reached up and patted the furry face. When Hawkman and Jennifer reached the spot, they gazed down at dirty frightened features. Immediately, the small person sat up and tried to scoot away on her buttocks, but she grimaced and agony showed in the turned down mouth.

"Don't be scared; we're not going to hurt you," Hawkman said, leaning toward the child.

She stared at him with wide eyes.

"Don't be alarmed by my eye-patch. I injured my eye a long time ago and have to protect it from the bright sunlight."

Jennifer stared at the small frame and her gaze traveled down the body, then she pointed. "She's injured. Look at her swollen ankle. It's either broken or very badly sprained." Jennifer reached down to touch the flesh, but the girl slapped away her hand. "Are you in much pain?"

The girl nodded, but didn't say a word. Instead she put both arms around the dog and buried her head in the fur.

Jennifer walked around and sat down on the log beside the animal. "Your dog brought us to you. She knew you needed help."

Pulling her face away from the canine's fur, she pointed at the dog and glanced at Jennifer.

"Yes, she found us out riding along the trail and barked for us to come. We knew she wanted something, but had no idea her mistress was in trouble."

The girl gave the lab a big hug.

"Can you talk?" Jennifer asked.

The girl shook her head.

"Yet, you can hear and understand what we're saying?"

She gave several big nods.

"Where do you live?" Hawkman asked. "We need to let your parents know where you are."

Fear enveloped the child's features and she shook her head violently.

"Don't you want us to take you home?" he asked.

She made fists out of both her hands and made the motions of being hit all over her body.

"Did you run from them so you wouldn't be beat?"

She shrugged her shoulders and waved her hands.

"I don't understand," Hawkman said.

Grabbing a twig, she cleared off a patch of ground and drew some stick figures, a house, and more figures inside. Jennifer and Hawkman studied the drawing but couldn't make heads or tails of it.

"Can you write your name?" Jennifer asked.

The girl immediately cleared off the picture she'd drawn and wrote 'Babs'.

Jennifer smiled. "Babs?"

She nodded.

"Babs, how about coming home with us? You can draw on a piece of paper and maybe we can figure out what you're trying to tell us." Jennifer said.

She again wrote in the dirt. "OK".

Jennifer glanced up at Hawkman. "Do you think you could carry her to the four-wheeler or do you want to bring it to her? We've got to get Babs to a doctor."

"She doesn't look like she weighs much."

Jennifer looked back at the girl. "My name is Jennifer and this is Tom, my husband. He's going to lift you and take you to our Polaris, so don't be afraid."

She pointed to the dog.

"Yes, she can come too."

Hawkman picked up the girl. "She's light as a feather."

They made their way back to the four-wheeler, the dog jogging alongside. Hawkman placed Babs on the area behind the driver, where she straddled the machine. Jennifer climbed on behind her, and Hawkman climbed onto the seat. He started it up and turned around, then slowly headed back up the hill. Jennifer hung onto the girl, especially when she noticed her wincing in pain. Babs' long, light brown hair kept blowing into Jennifer's face, but she avoided it as much as possible.

Jennifer moved the girl's arms toward Hawkman's waist. "Hold onto Tom if you feel you're going to fall."

Even though Hawkman crept along, Babs grimaced as they bounced over the rough terrain. Jennifer noticed Babs grabbed Hawkman's belt and grit her teeth. Soon they were on smoother ground and the girl relaxed her hold, but didn't let go. The dog ran beside the four-wheeler, never letting Babs out of her sight.

As they approached the houses, Babs twisted her head and stared at each one as they passed. When Hawkman pulled into their driveway and brought the Polaris to a stop, Babs removed her grip from his belt and started to get off, but Jennifer stopped her.

"Don't try. Tom will carry you inside, then we'll take you to see a doctor. We've got to find out how badly you're hurt."

Hawkman carried the girl into the house and placed her on the couch. Jennifer made sure Babs' bad leg rested on the cushions. She noticed the ankle had swollen more, so she made an ice pack and handed it to her.

"Hold this on your ankle for about fifteen minutes; take if off for a while, then put it on another area."

Babs took the ice and nodded.

Hawkman motioned for Jennifer to come into the kitchen. "If we take her into town to the hospital, the Child Services will take control since we're not the parents."

Jennifer frowned. "I hadn't thought about that, but bet you're right, and we'll never find out why she ran away." She gripped

Hawkman's arm. "What are we going to do? A doctor needs to examine her ankle, it's really swollen."

"How about we run her up the road to my hunting partner, Doctor Wilson. He's retired from the medical profession, but I'm sure he'd take a look at it."

"Splendid idea. However, I don't think we should tell him her story. Why don't we just say she's visiting us and we took her out to show off the eagle's nest. In her excitement, she jumped off the four-wheeler and turned her ankle."

"Sounds good, but you'll need to tell Babs why we're lying."

"I have an uncanny feeling she'll be okay with it."

They both walked into the living room. Hawkman stood back and observed the child's reaction when Jennifer mentioned the Child Services. The girl's eyes filled with horror. After listening to the rest of Jennifer's narrative, her facial features relaxed and she smiled while nodding vigorously.

Hawkman went outside to move the four-wheeler and back out the SUV from the garage.

Jennifer patted Babs on the uninjured leg. "The doctor will probably have to cut the leg of your jeans. If we're lucky he'll go up the seam and I can mend them. You and I are about the same size, so I'll give you some clothes to wear when we get back. In fact, I'll take a pair of shorts in case he has to do more damage to your clothes." The girl needed a bath and a complete clean outfit, but they didn't have time.

Hawkman poked his head in the door. "You gals ready?"

"Yes, put Babs into the SUV. I'll be right out," Jennifer said, as she scurried to the bedroom, grabbed shorts, and a tee shirt, then stuffed the items into a duffle bag. When she climbed in, she laughed. "I see we have an extra passenger. You're a real softy."

The big Golden lab lay on the floor with her head on the seat, looking up at Babs with soulful eyes. Babs gave her pet a reassuring pat on her head.

Hawkman grinned. "I didn't have much of a choice. The minute I had Babs on the seat with her leg up, the dog leaped in and wasn't about to leave her mistress."

Jennifer opened the passenger side door. "Before we leave, let me get the leash I found on the road. I knew it would come in handy one of these days, and I know right where it is." She jumped out, dashed into the house and ran back within seconds.

They were soon on their way up the road to Doctor Wilson's house. Jennifer turned in her seat so she could talk to Babs. "Are you doing okay?"

She nodded.

Jennifer handed her a pad of paper and a pen. "What's your dog's name? Does she mind a leash?"

After she wrote on it, she handed it back.

Jennifer smiled. "Lucy, I like that.'

The dog perked up her ears and barked. Everyone laughed.

"Oh, good, she doesn't mind a leash. The doctor might not want an animal in his house, so one of us can stay outside with her."

They soon drove up a long driveway. Hawkman pulled up in front of the house and stopped the 4x4. "I'll make sure he's here and will look at her."

He soon came out and lifted Babs from the SUV. Before he carried her inside, she gave the dog some hand signals. Jennifer snapped the leash onto the dog's thin collar. Lucy whined, but sat down on her haunches beside Jennifer.

CHAPTER FOUR

Hawkman came back outside. "Why don't you go with her; I think she'd be more comfortable. I explained to Doctor Wilson about Babs not speaking, and as our guest she had tripped running to see the eagle nests."

Jennifer handed him the leash, and joined Babs in the doctor's small home office. She had a clipboard in her hands and was filling out a form. Jennifer realized she knew nothing about the girl, so she looked over Babs' shoulder as she wrote. She learned her full name was Barbara Ann Jones, fourteen years of age; her parents were Luke and Annie. They lived at County Road, Box 1623, Montague, CA 96064.

Babs held up the form to Jennifer, and pointed to some empty blanks. Jennifer took it and wrote 'not applicable' on the rest of the questions; then she handed it to the doctor.

"Tom and I will pay the bill."

He smiled. "Jennifer, I'm not the least bit concerned about money right now."

She'd always liked Doctor Wilson and studied his appearance as he glanced over the information. He'd put on weight, but she figured it had occurred since his retirement. His unruly gray hair hung across his forehead like it had a mind of its own. The wrinkles around his blue eyes turned up like the smile wrinkles around his mouth when he spoke to Babs in a soft, caring voice.

"Looks mighty sore," he said, touching Babs ankle.

She grimaced.

"This might be a little uncomfortable, but bear with me and maybe I can find out if it's broken." He poked and probed before finally looking up at Babs. "You doing okay?"

She nodded.

"You're being very brave. I don't think you've broken any bones, but I can't be sure without an x-ray. Since I don't have a machine, I'm going to make arrangements at a clinic in Yreka on Monday. Meanwhile, I'll treat this as a second degree ankle sprain. We'll know in a couple of days if it's anything worse." He glanced down at the thong on her good foot and gestured. "Were you wearing those?"

She ducked her head and nodded.

He rolled his eyes and looked at the ceiling. "No wonder you've ended up with such a bad sprain. If there are no bones broken, you're very lucky"

After wrapping the ankle in an elastic bandage, he handed her several sheets of instructions. "I've got a set of crutches I'm going to lend you. The Caseys can return them later. You won't want to put any weight on that foot for several days. Keep it elevated above your heart level when you're sitting until the swelling goes down and the pain subsides. It could take a few days."

He walked over to a closet and pulled out the aluminum crutches. "I'll adjust these to fit you." He had her hold onto his shoulder as she stood on her good foot while he fixed them to her size.

"Mrs. Casey, I don't think she'll need anything stronger than a Tylenol for pain. Apply ice every four to six hours if she's real uncomfortable; otherwise, call me."

He stood. "If the swelling hasn't gone down in a couple of days, come back and see me." He patted Babs on the shoulder. "When you're running through the forest, please make sure you're wearing boots."

Babs smiled and nodded.

Jennifer carried the crutches and went outside where Hawkman and Lucy were waiting. She took the leash. "You can go get her, we're through."

When he carried the girl out, the dog yipped and bounced; she was happy to see her mistress, but seemed to know better than to jump on her.

Jennifer gave Hawkman a quick rundown of the prognosis as they strolled toward the SUV. Once they got Babs situated in the 4X4, with the crutches at her side and Lucy on the floorboard, Jennifer climbed into the passenger side.

Within minutes they arrived at their house. Hawkman carried Babs into the living room and put her on the couch. Lucy stood at the door whining. "Is Lucy house broken?"

She nodded.

"I'll get an old rug for her to lay on; this way she can be near you. She won't be happy outside."

"Put it in the guest room," Jennifer called from the master bedroom. "I'm getting Babs a pair of pajamas to wear. It's getting late; we're all exhausted and hungry."

The doctor had cut Babs' jeans up the seam to a little above her knee, so Jennifer figured she could sew it up real easily. First, the girl's clothes had to be washed, as they were filthy.

Babs maneuvered the crutches very well and made her way to the bathroom where Jennifer had placed the pajamas, a towel, washcloth and bar of soap on the counter. "I'll get you some fresh clothes in the morning, right now, I'm going to fix sandwiches, then we'll get ready for a good night's sleep. Put all the clothes you have on into this paper sack and I'll launder them tomorrow."

Lucy was already on the rug Hawkman had placed in the room. She waited patiently for her mistress as Jennifer turned back the bed and placed pillows at the foot so Babs could elevate her leg.

When Babs entered the room on the crutches, Jennifer smiled. "My goodness, you look like a new and pretty person with all that dirt gone. You go ahead and climb into bed; I'll bring your sandwich in here. You need to get that leg elevated with some ice on it."

Babs smiled and did as told.

"Does Lucy eat leftovers? I'm sure she's hungry and since we don't own a dog, that's all I have."

Babs nodded, gave Lucy some hand signals, and the lab followed Jennifer to the kitchen. Jennifer filled a paper plate with meat scraps and placed a bowl of water beside it on the floor. The dog drank all the water, then gobbled down the food.

"My goodness, girl, you were certainly thirsty and hungry," Jennifer said, as she patted the dog's back.

Lucy immediately went back to the guest room and lay down on her rug. Jennifer soon brought a sandwich on a tray, along with a bag of ice. When she turned to leave, the girl handed her a note. As Jennifer read it, tears welled in her eyes. The message said, 'Thank you for all you've done for Lucy and me.' "You're more than welcome," she said, leaving the room before her emotions overflowed.

When Jennifer returned to the guest room to pick up the tray, she found Babs
snuggled under the covers, sound asleep.

Jennifer and Hawkman lay in bed, talking softly.

"Did you notice how adorable she is?" Jennifer asked. "I love those deep dimples in her cheeks, set off by her cute turned up nose. Those big sparkly brown eyes would melt anyone's heart. Her hair hangs clear down almost to her hips."

"Yes, she's a cutie. Did she tell you about what happened?" he asked.

"Nothing, but tomorrow I will get her to tell me more. Right now I'm just thankful she didn't break a big bone in her ankle as that could have meant surgery."

"It puzzles me why she didn't want us to notify her parents. I have the feeling something dangerous happened to make her flee from home."

"I agree. Maybe we'll get some answers tomorrow."

"Hope so. We can't keep her forever."

"Turn over," Jennifer said. "I want to hug your back. I'm about to fall asleep."

"That's just because you're safer doing that than me hugging yours," Hawkman said.

Jennifer giggled. "Aw shucks, you've figured out my strategy."

CHAPTER FIVE

Sunday morning, Jennifer arose and placed typing paper on the kitchen bar along with a couple of number two pencil for Babs when she awoke. She wanted her to draw the reason she didn't want to go home.

Hawkman strolled in, tucking his shirt into his jeans. "Where's our patient?"

"She's not up yet."

He watched Jennifer as she put the skillet on the burner, and he rubbed his hands together. "Are we having a big breakfast this morning?"

She smiled. "Thought it might be pleasant since we have a guest."

About the time the bacon was crisp, Babs swung out of the room on her crutches with Lucy at her side. She went to the front door, let the dog out, then came over to Jennifer and pointed at her ankle.

"Wow, the swelling has really gone down. That's a good sign," Jennifer said. "However, you must still take it easy today, and don't put pressure on your ankle."

Babs nodded, then smiled at Hawkman.

Jennifer motioned toward the paper on the counter. "While I'm finishing breakfast, why don't you sketch what happened at your house yesterday. Take it into the living room and use the coffee table, but keep you foot elevated. I don't think it would be a good idea for you to sit on a bar stool with your leg dangling."

As soon as Babs settled on the couch, Lucy barked at the front door. Hawkman jumped off his seat. "I'll let her in."

The canine dashed inside, and immediately ran to the guest bedroom. Everyone laughed when she dragged the rug she'd slept on out into the living room, placed it next to her mistress and immediately sat down. Babs gave her a big hug.

"Now, she's one smart dog," Hawkman said.

"Uh, oh," Jennifer said. "Look who just poked her head around the corner."

Everyone looked toward the bedroom, and there stood Miss Marple. The hair stood on end along her humped back, and she hissed when she saw Lucy. Babs immediately made hand signals; the dog let out a little whine, went down on her belly and covered her nose with her paws.

Babs grinned as she watched the cat in her alert stance, slowly make her way to the hearth, where she leaped upon her favorite blanket, never taking her eyes off the dog.

"Miss Marple, you're still queen," Jennifer said, laughing.

Once they all ate, Babs handed Jennifer the sketch she'd made. After studying it, she gave it to Hawkman. "Tell me what you think, then I'll tell you my thoughts."

He sat down beside Babs and pointed to the drawing of a man and woman at the kitchen table. The woman had her mouth open as if she was screaming, and her hands were held up in the air. "Is this your mom and dad?"

Babs nodded.

Two men, whom Babs had drawn with bandanas around their faces and guns in their hands, were standing inside the door of her house.

He pointed to them. "These men barged into your house. Where were you?"

She wrote, 'outside playing with Lucy'.

"Did they come in a car or truck?"

She shook her head, and continued writing. 'I saw them coming out of the woods, acting funny, all hunched down like hiding. They headed right toward our house. I ducked behind some bushes and peeked in the window'.

"Tell me what they did?"

Babs continued writing. 'One of them tied Dad up, while the other one pointed a gun at Mom and told her to fix them some food or he'd kill Dad'.

"Did you know these men?"

Again she shook her head and wrote. 'Never saw them in my life'.

"Did they have their faces covered?" he asked.

'I just put them with masks, so you'd know they were the bad guys.'

Hawkman glanced at Jennifer sitting in her chair, taking in every word. "Sounds like we have a problem here."

Jennifer leaned toward Babs. "While we were out in the woods, we heard a scream; sounded like 'run baby run'. Did it come from your mother?"

The girl nodded and again wrote on the paper. 'The guy thought Mom was talking to her chickens, as she told him she needed to get a bucket of water before she could cook, and he let her leave the house. Then he ran outside when she yelled for me to run. I heard her telling him a hawk was after her baby chicks. The guy was dumb enough to believe her, so she just went ahead and drew water from the well.'

"Your mother sounds like quite a woman," Jennifer said.

Babs wrote. 'She is'. Then she placed the paper on the table and wiped away the tears running down her cheeks.

"Oh, honey," Jennifer said, scooting next to her on the couch, and taking her into her arms. "Mr. Casey will figure out a way to save your folks from these horrible men."

She picked up the paper and quickly scribbled, 'What if they've already killed Mom and Pop?'

Hawkman moved so he stood in front of the girl. "Look at me, Babs. We don't know why these criminals are holding your parents. We need to contact the police." He looked over at Jennifer. "I'm going back to my office and make some phone calls."

He left the room and settled at his desk, then scooted his personal directory toward himself, and opened it to Detective Bud Chandler. Fortunately, he had his office and private phone numbers. He'd try the work one first. After dialing, he pushed the speaker phone.

"Detective Chandler."

"Hi, Bud, this is Tom Casey."

"Since you're calling the office, this obviously isn't an invite to dinner."

Hawkman laughed. "No, but in the future we'll get together. I wanted to ask if you're looking for a couple of men, either escaped from jail, or did something unlawful?"

"How'd you know?"

Hawkman quickly briefed him about the story Babs had told them. "The child is mute, but she drew pictures of what had happened to her yesterday. Jennifer and I came to the conclusion these men were running from the law."

"Can the girl describe them?"

"Probably, but we didn't go into the description yet. The child is very fearful they have killed her parents."

"How good of an artist is she?"

"Fair-to-middling. She's only fourteen, but who knows how long she's been sketching her answers."

"She's at your house?"

"Yes."

"You think she'll draw for me?"

"I'll prepare her for the big scary man before you get here."

Chandler laughed. "Thanks. I'll be out in about an hour."

Hawkman hung up, and walked back into the living room. "Babs, do you think you could draw some head pictures of those two guys?"

She nodded.

"Good, because Detective Chandler will be here in about an hour and it would really help him."

She frowned and wrote on her paper pad. 'Who?'

"He's a part of the police force in Yreka, and he might be able to tell us more about these two men if you can made a good sketch. He'll be the man who will help us save your parents. You'll like him."

Babs wrote a note to Jennifer. 'I need to change clothes before he gets here.'

"Of course." She glanced at her husband. "Hawkman, why don't you take Lucy outside for a few minutes while Babs changes clothes. Give the dog a little exercise, I'm sure she needs it."

"Sure. Come on Lucy, let's go outside and play."

The dog looked at her mistress. Babs gave her the gesture to go, and the dog jumped up and ran out the door with Hawkman.

Babs cocked her head and wrote on the paper. 'Why did you call your husband 'Hawkman'?'

Jennifer grinned. "That's his nickname. I'll tell you how he got it after we get you dressed."

Babs slipped into a pair of shorts and tee shirt Jennifer furnished. "Those fit you pretty darn good. I think I better tighten up that elastic bandage around your ankle, it's falling down a bit."

The child grimaced once and pointed to the big bruise on her leg. Jennifer loosened the bandage a bit. Once the girl was dressed and comfortable, Jennifer went back to the bedroom and retrieved a hairbrush she no longer used, along with a hand mirror. When she came back into the living room, she couldn't believe her eyes. Miss Marple sat like a queen on Babs' lap.

CHAPTER SIX

Jennifer stopped in her tracks and smiled. "She must really like you. Seldom does Miss Marple take to strangers."

Hawkman's voice came through the front door. "Is it safe to come in?"

"One moment," Jennifer called, as she swooped up her pet and put her on the hearth. "Okay."

Lucy came bounding in, and Miss Marple hunched her back and hissed.

Jennifer glanced at Babs as she handed her the hair brush and mirror. "I didn't want the cat on your lap when Lucy came in. She might have scratched you."

Once Babs finished brushing her locks, she began working on the sketches of the two men who'd invaded her home. Jennifer had furnished her with a clipboard and soon, the girl placed the drawings on the coffee table.

Hawkman came out of the kitchen with a mug of coffee and picked up one of the portraits. "Very good, Babs. I think if either of these men are wanted by Detective Chandler, he'll recognize them from these."

Hearing the crunch on the gravel driveway, Hawkman checked out the kitchen window. "He's here."

Hawkman stepped out the front door as the six foot, burly detective unfolded himself from under the steering wheel, and another officer climbed out of the passenger side of the unmarked patrol car.

Chandler gestured toward him. "Tom Casey, meet my chief assistant Officer Owens."

"Good meeting you," Hawkman said, as they shook hands.

They stood beside the car, and Chandler rested his hip against the fender. "You told me this young girl is mute, but can hear, write and draw."

Hawkman nodded. "Yes."

"How long has she been mute?"

"I have no idea."

Chandler rubbed his chin. "Sounds like she's had some trauma in her life."

"Very possible," Hawkman said. "I've gotten the impression her family is poor."

"She's obviously had some education, if she knows how to write."

"True, or home schooled," Hawkman said.

Chandler stepped toward the front entry. "I'm eager to meet her."

Hawkman raised a hand. "Before we go inside, there's a favor I need to ask."

"Sure, shoot."

"We'd like the girl to stay here with us. We sure don't want the Child Services to come, take her away, and put her into some foster home that wouldn't understand the ordeal she's going through. Can you help us there?"

Chandler reached over and patted him on the arm. "No worry, I'll see to it that no one will take her out of your home."

"Thanks." Hawkman led them inside. Babs turned and stared at the two strangers as they moved in front of her. Lucy let out a quick bark before Babs signaled the animal to be quiet.

"Babs, this is Detective Chandler and Officer Owens. Show them the sketches of the two men who barged into your home."

She held out the two pictures to Chandler. He took them, and with only one glance, nodded, then showed them to the officer.

"Yep, those are the two," Owens said.

Babs scribbled on her pad of paper and handed it to the detective. "Are they dangerous?" her note read.

"Unfortunately, yes," he said, noting the fear laden expression on the girl's face as her eyes filled with tears.

Jennifer quickly moved onto the couch next to Babs, and put an arm around her shoulders. "That doesn't mean they've harmed your parents. I'm sure the detective and his men will go to your house to check on them."

Detective Chandler blushed, glanced at Jennifer, then spoke softly to Babs. "I didn't mean to frighten you."

"She's the kind of girl who'd want to know the truth, even if it scares her."

The detective knelt down in front of Babs. "I'm sure this whole ordeal has you very concerned about your folks."

She scribbled another note and handed it to Chandler.

He looked at Jennifer. "She wants to know what these men have done. Should I tell her?"

"Yes," Jennifer said. "Now that she knows they're dangerous, don't keep her in the dark."

The detective took a deep breath. "These two men," he pointed at the pictures she'd drawn, "each brandished guns as they entered a bank in Yreka. The customers and cashiers were ordered to lay on the floor while they stole several thousand dollars from behind the counter. However, before they could get into the vault, one of the customers had managed to call 911 on his cell phone, and the police soon arrived. When the crooks saw the patrol cars through the large windows, they grabbed a young woman as a hostage. We couldn't take the chance of firing because of the situation. They jumped into a car and fortunately, pushed the girl out a few miles down the road. She was unharmed except for a few scrapes and bruises. We found the stolen vehicle abandoned in the park, and aren't sure if there was another person involved who picked them up at a certain point, or they took off on foot."

Babs wrote a quick note. "Did they shoot anyone?"

Chandler shook his head. "No. You say there were only two men who entered your home?"

"That's all I saw," she scribbled.

Jennifer walked over with a handful of papers. "Here are the written notes from Babs, telling exactly what she saw."

The detective took a few minutes and read through them, then looked at Hawkman.
"Do you know where the girl lives?"

"Have a good idea, but not positive." He turned toward Babs. "You were just on the edge of a trail when we found you. If we followed the path, would it lead us to your home?"

She nodded, and wrote. "You'd come to the backside of the house."

"Can a truck or car get to the front?"

She scribbled again. "Yes. On Country Road."

Hawkman went back to his office, retrieved the county map, and spread it out on the dining room table. He ran his finger along a line showing Chandler where he and Jennifer had found the injured girl. "This map doesn't show the path, but I know where it is. This route requires a four-wheel drive, very steep and rough." He looked closer and put his finger on the map. "Here's Country Road. Looks like it's not paved."

Chandler wrote down the cross roads on a sheet of paper. "I'm going to need back-up, and might even need the Swat team. Should get moving on this ASAP." The detective walked over to the couch and patted Babs on the shoulder. "We're going to see if we can't get these crooks and set your parents free."

She grabbed her pencil and wrote a big 'Thank you' on a sheet of paper.

"I'm going to take your notes and sketches with me. I'll give them back later. Now, I have to go back to the station and get things rolling."

Hawkman accompanied the detective and Officer Owens to their vehicle, then leaned against the car. "I'd like you to deputize me so I could help out on this case."

Chandler looked at him and grinned. "Thought you'd never ask. You're deputized." Then he pointed a finger at him. "Don't do anything until I get back."

Hawkman put both hands up in front of him. "I won't, but with my Polaris we can go in the back way. So keep that idea in your plans. We can hit them from the front and back. Let's just pray Babs' folks are still alive."

CHAPTER SEVEN

Not sure what to tell Babs about the plans, Hawkman delayed going into the house, instead went to the lean-to where he'd parked the Polaris. He checked it over and found the machine in tiptop condition; it was ready to roll.

He finally wandered into the kitchen, and avoided looking at the young girl, but could feel her gaze penetrating his back. Opening the refrigerator, he removed three sodas and went into the living room where he handed one to Babs; she mouthed 'thank you' and he gave one to Jennifer.

"Thanks," she said. "So what's the next step?"

Hawkman settled into his chair, flipped up his eye-patch and rubbed his eyes. "When Chandler returns from rounding up his men, he and I will make our way down the backside, while the rest of the officers go to the front. We'll survey the home, and see if we can figure out what's going on."

He leaned forward and rested his elbows on his thighs. "Babs, what type of vehicle do your folks drive, and where is it normally kept?"

She quickly jotted, 'Old dark blue Ford pickup; usually in shed next to the house, if not out front.'

"Could you sketch a picture of your dad? We want to make sure we don't mistake him for one of the criminals."

She nodded and immediately picked up a sheet of paper.

When a loud squawk came from the aviary, Hawkman jerked his head around. "Bet Pretty Girl needs food and water."

Jennifer wagged a finger at him. "You've neglected her the last couple of days."

He hopped up and headed for the deck. Babs watched intently through the window as he opened the door of a large cage.

She wrote a note to Jennifer. 'What's out there?'

"His pet falcon, Pretty Girl. He takes her into the field about three times a month and lets her hunt. If he can't take her out, he makes sure she has a mouse or other food she likes."

Babs made a face. 'How does he take her hunting? Doesn't she fly away?' she scribbled.

"So far, no. He carries her on his arm, which he protects from her sharp talons with a long leather glove. She mounts his arm and he takes her out to the middle of a field where the falcon takes off into the forest to search for a prey. Once she's eaten, she flies back to him."

'When my ankle heals, can I see her?' she wrote.

"Sure. Mr. Casey might even take you with him when he takes her hunting."

The girl beamed, then held up the sketch she'd made of her father.

"Excellent, Babs," Jennifer said. "You're drawing makes him look alive. They won't have any problem knowing who he is."

Hawkman walked back into the house. "The little stinker showed her unhappiness with me; nipped my hand hard enough to bring blood."

"She's punishing you for not giving her any attention. I'll get a Band-Aid," Jennifer said, heading for the bathroom.

Hawkman washed the deep scratch and swabbed it with an ointment, then plastered a couple of bandages over it. Jennifer showed him the drawing Babs had made of her dad.

Hawkman studied the full body sketch: short and stocky, cane in a large hand, pug nose, rim of hair around his head, a big smile showing one eyetooth missing, and squinting eyes. He glanced at Babs who was biting her lower lip as she stared at him. "Very good. Does he always carry the cane?"

She nodded, and wrote. 'He has a very bad limp.'

"I'll show this to Detective Chandler when he gets here."

Hawkman paced the floor between the kitchen and dining room. Soon he spotted the detective's unmarked car and two patrol vehicles coming over the bridge. Chandler pulled into the driveway and the others continued west. Hawkman took the drawing off the counter and walked outside.

Chandler scooted out of the car. "My team is going to the front of the house. Had a good map at work that showed better detail of the roads than yours. Even showed the back trail we'll be taking."

"Good," Hawkman said and handed him the sketch. "Here's what Luke Jones looks like. Don't want to mistake him for one of the thugs."

The detective sat back down on the edge of the car seat and used his dispatch radio to notify his team of the description of Babs' father. He then glanced up at Hawkman. "Are you ready to go?"

"Yep."

"Okay, let's hit it."

The two men climbed onto the Polaris and took off. When they reached the path where Babs and her dog were found, Hawkman turned onto it, but only went to the edge of the trees and parked in a thicket.

"I don't know how close the house is, and this four-wheeler is so loud we could give ourselves away. Let's go the rest of the way on foot," Hawkman said, climbing off the machine.

"Good idea," Chandler said. "This thing is not only noisy, but a rough ride."

Hawkman grinned. "Babs said the trail leads to the back of her house."

"That's where we want to be."

The men stayed in the shadows of the large trees as they followed the trail. Hawkman caught a glimpse of the roof of a building through the forest, raised a hand, and pointed ahead. They stepped deeper into the trees as they approached, keeping as quiet as possible. The floor of the woods was littered with dead branches, along with a heavy coat of crackling leaves, making it very difficult to continue silently. Soon they came to the edge of the clearing where they squatted behind some brush and could view the rear of the rustic log cabin.

"Seems mighty still," Chandler whispered.

"Do you think your men are here yet?"

The detective checked his watch. "Doubt it. Their route is a bit longer, and probably as bumpy as the back trail. They'll park about a half mile down the road and go the rest of the distance by foot. I don't want to call them on the walkie-talkie as it squawks and would give away their location."

"Understood," Hawkman said in a low voice. "What about the Swat Team?"

"They're on call, if we need them. They know how to get here."

Hawkman pointed to a shed. "I'm going to see if I can check that outbuilding. Babs said her dad had an old pickup he used and parked it in the shed or at the front of the house."

Chandler nodded. "I've got you covered."

Hawkman disappeared into the trees and made his way toward the hut. Coming upon the rear side with weeds as tall as the roof, he noticed a small door with a window. He tried looking through the glass, but it had so much dirt on it, he couldn't see a thing. Trying the door knob, he found it either securely locked or so warped it wouldn't budge. He took a chance and peeked around the corner. He could see the front of the cabin, but no vehicle. It unsettled him that the place appeared so abnormally quiet, except for the chickens running around in a fenced area behind the cabin. Even they seemed subdued.

The detective moved up behind Hawkman. "My men are here. We're going to charge the house."

Hawkman noticed movement in the brush around the property. One at a time, the officers dashed toward the cabin with guns drawn, then flattened themselves against the walls. He thought it odd that nothing happened. Taking a chance, he darted around the shed and flung open the double doors. No pickup rested on the dirt floor.

The two officers one each side of the cabin's front door, kicked it open and went inside. One of them stuck his head out and called for Detective Chandler. Hawkman, thinking the worst, made his heart skip a beat. He prayed Babs' parents were alive.

CHAPTER EIGHT

Hawkman trotted behind the detective into the cabin, and stepped quickly toward the groaning person tied up in a chair. Blood had dried on the man's face from a gash in his forehead. Holding onto the hefty male, Hawkman quickly untied the ropes. "Are you okay and is your name Luke Jones?"

"Yes, to both questions." He rubbed his arms, glanced around the room at the officers, and gasped. "You've got to find the two men who took my Annie, and I don't know where my daughter is."

Chandler stepped up to the man. "I'm Detective Chandler, and we'll definitely try to find your wife."

"Babs is safe," Hawkman assured him. "She injured an ankle running away, but she's fine and is with my wife."

"Can you tell us what happened here?" Chandler asked.

"Out of nowhere, these two men crashed into my house, brandishing guns. I tried swinging at them with my cane. They yanked it away, and walloped me across the head, causing me to fall down. They yanked me up, then slammed me down on the chair and tied me up. They ordered my wife to fix them food. When she went outside to get water from the well, I heard her yell, 'run Babs run'. She's a brave woman, my Annie."

The detective removed from his pocket the folded sketches Babs had made of the two criminals. "Do you recognize these men?"

Luke pointed. "Yes, they're the ones who barged in here." He raised a brow. "Those look like my daughter's drawings."

"They are. She saw them heading for the cabin." Chandler folded the pictures and returned them to his pocket. "I'm assuming your wife fixed them a meal; then what happened?" Chandler asked.

"After hogging it down, they wanted to know where I stored my vehicle. I told them I had an old pickup in the shed, but it wouldn't run long if you didn't baby it. They wanted the keys, then grabbed Annie and pushed her out the door. Told me I wouldn't see her again if I told the cops."

"How long were they here?"

"Not more than two hours."

"Did you see which direction they went?"

"No, sir, I just heard the truck start up. It sounded like they headed down the driveway. I have no idea which way they turned on the main road. Regardless, they won't get far as there wasn't much gas in the pickup. Even if they poured in the extra gallon can's worth, that old engine sucks it up like water." He hit the tip of the cane on the wood floor. "I pray they don't take it out on Annie when the truck stops."

"We need to get you to the hospital."

"Naw, I don't need to see a doctor. I've had worse than this ding on my head, and did fine tending to it myself."

"Maybe so, but I'd feel better if you were checked," Chandler said. "We'll bring a patrol car to the front. Do you think you can walk?"

"Yeah, just hand me my cane." He pointed to the floor. "Can one of your men bring me back. The chickens have to be looked after."

"Yes," the detective said, as he ordered one of the officers to go get the car. "Take Mr. Jones to the hospital, wait for him, then bring him home."

After getting Luke Jones loaded into the car and on the way, Hawkman and Chandler went through the small log cabin looking for any clues they might find. The detective placed some plates and utensils into a plastic bag. "I hope these might yield some prints or DNA."

Hawkman observed the cabin had no running water, and only one small light bulb hanging bare in the middle of the room. The cabin consisted of two bedrooms and one large main area which held a wood burning stove, a small refrigerator, rustic table and chairs for three, along with a couch, a couple of overstuffed worn chairs and a small round oak table. The place appeared neat and clean.

In the small bedroom, which Hawkman assumed belonged to Babs', were books, ranging from math, science, art and fiction. It made him wonder where the girl had been educated. She appeared up to par in her studies.

When the two men finished inside, they went outside where the two officers were closing off the area around the shed with yellow police tape.

"I think we need to bring the tech guys out, so they can take some casts of the tire treads and shoe prints," said one of the officers.

"Good idea, get them on the phone," said Chandler

Once arrangements were made with the lab people, Chandler turned to Hawkman. "It'll soon be dark. Let's get back to your place so I can get my car."

"Sure," Hawkman said.

Before climbing onto the Polaris, he ordered his officers to remain there for the lab crew and he'd be back shortly to join them.

Hawkman fired up the four-wheeler and drove uphill most of the way until they soon arrived at his place. Chandler hopped into his unmarked vehicle.

"I'll give you a call tomorrow," the detective said, and took off.

When Hawkman walked into the house, Babs gazed at him with anxiety in her eyes. He walked over and stood before her. "Your dad is fine. He's at the hospital getting checked over. I don't know if they'll keep him overnight or not."

'Did they hurt him?' she scribbled.

"Not bad, a conk on the head with his own cane. He'll probably need a stitch or two."

She quickly wrote, 'What about my Mom?'

He took a deep breath. "We don't know. Your dad said the two men took her with them in his truck. It appears to be a hostage situation, as they threatened your dad if he notified the police."

Babs put a hand over her mouth and tears spilled over her cheeks. Jennifer quickly slid onto the couch and held her in her arms.

"Mr. Casey and the police will do everything possible to find your mom," Jennifer said, as she rocked the girl.

Lucy, sensing something wrong, stood up and put her head on Babs' leg. Looking up at her owner with soulful eyes, the dog whined softly. Babs gave her a hug, then picked up her pen again, 'When can I see my Dad?'

"Unfortunately, you don't have a phone, so we won't know if they dismissed him from the hospital tonight. I tell you what. After you get your ankle x-rayed tomorrow, I'll take you to your house."

She nodded in agreement. Wiping tears from her cheeks, she wrote on the pad again and held it up to Jennifer. 'Can we go early?'

"As soon as you're ready in the morning," Jennifer said, as she moved away from the girl.

"Babs, should I go fasten the chickens up?" Hawkman asked.

She scratched her pen across the paper. 'They usually go into the henhouse at night. We just shut the door so no varmint can get inside and eat them. They'll probably be okay this one time.'

***

Monday morning, Jennifer and Babs took off for the clinic Dr. Wilson had recommended. The nurse ushered Babs into the x-ray room in a wheelchair. Jennifer sat in the waiting room. When they brought the girl out, the woman asked if they could wait a few minutes for the results.

A man in a white jacket appeared and called for them to follow. Once settled in his office he took the x-ray and put it on a light panel.

"I'm Dr. Tully. Dr. Wilson asked that I examine your x-ray and let you know the results. I have good news. No bones are broken, and it appears it's not as bad as Dr. Wilson thought. You've obviously iced and stayed off the injured foot. He said he'd lent you crutches, so my advice is to continue to use them. I'm going to rewrap the ankle and if all goes well, you should be as good as new in a couple of weeks. If you sense any change for the worse, come back and see me."

   After the doctor wrapped Babs' ankle, they were on their way back to Copco Lake. Jennifer noticed Babs stared out the window most of the way home. She knew the girl worried about her parents, especially her mother.

CHAPTER NINE

When Hawkman heard Jennifer's vehicle, he went to the door and stepped outside. Babs climbed out of the SUV, put the crutches under her arms and swung toward him. Lucy had bounded out of the house, barked a greeting, and ran circles around her mistress.

"Good news," Jennifer said. "No broken bones and the sprain is not as bad as we thought. Babs should be good as new in a couple of weeks."

Hawkman gave the girl a thumbs up. "Detective Chandler called to inform us that your father is at home. They didn't keep him at the hospital, because he just needed a couple of stitches. Also, they're searching the area for your dad's truck. I'm sorry, there's been no word on your mom."

Babs ducked her head and bit her lower lip.

"Do you want me to take you to see your dad?" Hawkman asked.

The girl nodded, and turned toward his vehicle. Lucy followed and jumped inside when Babs opened the back door.

Hawkman glanced at Jennifer. "You want to go?"

"No, you go ahead. I don't think she's going to want to come back here. She'll choose to stay with her dad. Hold on a minute and let me grab her clean clothes."

"I'm sure you're right," Hawkman said, as he climbed into the driver's seat.

Jennifer dashed out of the house with a brown paper sack, and handed it to Babs.

"Be sure to use your crutches. I'll return them to Dr. Wilson when you're able to walk without their aid."

Babs nodded and mouthed 'thank you'.

Lucy gave a hearty bark, wagged her tail, and gave Jennifer a wet kiss on her hand as she patted the girl's arm. Stepping out of the way so Hawkman could back out of the driveway, Jennifer waved.

Turning toward the bridge, Hawkman pointed at the dark clouds. "Looks like we might have a storm moving in."

It took a few minutes longer to go the front route, but he soon made it to the Jones' cabin. Luke limped out of the house using his cane. When he saw Babs and Lucy, a big grin covered his face

"It's so good to see my girl," he said, wrapping his child in a big bear hug. "Come in, Mr. Casey."

Hawkman walked in behind the two and Luke motioned for him to have a seat.

Luke's smile disappeared as he turned toward Hawkman. "Have you heard anything about my Annie?"

"No, but I can assure you the police are looking. So far, they haven't found your truck or your wife. I will definitely let you know of any news. I will be joining the hunt this afternoon."

Luke rubbed a hand over his face, then glanced at Babs as she headed out the back door on her crutches. "So tell me the story about my little girl."

Hawkman gave him a quick rundown of how they found Babs with a sprained ankle.

Luke reached over and patted Lucy. "She's a very smart dog, and never lets Babs out of her sight. Thank you for taking her to the doctor. What do I owe you for the visit?"

Hawkman shook his head. "Nothing." Standing, he stuck his thumbs in his back jeans pockets. "Mr. Jones, how are you going to go to town for supplies, if you have no vehicle?"

"Fortunately, the wife and I had just been to the store the day before those men broke into our home. So right now, I have no need to go."

"I'll stop by now and then until we find your pickup. I also worry about you having no phone."

"Too expensive for the little we'd use it. As you know, our Babs doesn't speak due to the accident she witnessed as a little girl. Neither Annie or I had any use for one until now."

Hawkman frowned. "What accident?"

"It happened when she was just four years old, and we lived in the city. She and Annie were standing on the curb waiting for the cars to pass before crossing the street. A truck turned the corner and flipped over in front of them. A bloody body was thrown at their feet. Babs never spoke another word."

"A horrifying experience for a little girl to see," Hawkman said.

Luke nodded. "We took her to a therapist, but no one seemed to help; so we let it be. Maybe one of these days she'll find her voice again."

"She seems to be educated, so she has obviously done well in school."

"Yep," Luke said. "Babs is as smart as a whip. She catches the school bus down the road a bit. I don't think she's missed over two days in the past seven years. She's already looking forward to the start of the next term."

"Mr. Jones, I'm taking off now. I'll check in with you periodically and see if you need anything. I'll also keep you informed about your wife."

"Please call me Luke." He bowed his head. "I appreciate your concern. I just pray they haven't hurt my Annie."

Hawkman patted the man's shoulder and left.

***

Babs made her way to her favorite spot in the back yard. A large limb had fallen from the big oak tree years ago and made a perfect seat in the shade. She leaned the crutches against the bark and sat down. Lucy dropped at her feet. Picking a dandelion, Babs twirled the seed laden plant between her fingers, then blew on the round fluff, scattering it across the ground. She knew it would just make more of them sprout, but right now she didn't care, as the worry over her mother had taken control of her mind and soul. She missed her something terrible and prayed the police would find her alive. It scared her to think those two horrible men had her in their clutches. What would they do to her? She shivered at the thought.

When her ankle grew stronger, she and Lucy would go looking for her mother. She knew these woods like the back of her hand. A crook would have a hard time hiding that pickup from her.

Before Dad had hurt his knee so bad, he'd taught her how to hunt, track and shoot a gun. She wouldn't tell him her plan, as he'd want to go, but he'd just slow her down, and she certainly didn't want to take the chance of him falling.

Lucy seemingly sensed her mistress' sadness, got up, grabbed a stick, plopped it in her lap, and waited for her to throw it. Babs laughed and tossed the twig. Lucy retrieved it and they continued with the game until Luke called for them to come inside. Babs tried to step with her bad ankle, but it still smarted, so she used the crutches.

Trying to be cheerful, Luke put his arm around Babs' shoulders. "One thing about it, my little girl, we won't starve as long as we have eggs from the chicken house, the smokehouse full of meat, and the garden."

She smiled.

"I'm not as good a cook as your mama, but I can scramble eggs and fry bacon. My stomach's been growling for some time, so we're eating a mite early. You and Lucy will have plenty of sunlight left to finish your game."

Babs went to the table and sat in her place. Lucy headed for the corner where she had an old rug, a bowl of water, and a plate for food. The dog knew better than to approach the table as she might just get whacked with a cane. After eating, Babs pointed to the wound on her dad's head.

"Quite a story there," he said. When those hoodlums barged into the house brandishing guns, I whacked one of them on the wrist with my cane and knocked the gun from his hand. He grabbed my stick and smacked me on the head with it. The police officer insisted I go to the hospital, which I didn't want to do. Anyway, they seemed to think I needed stitches."

Babs narrowed her eyes and a shiver ran down her spine at the thought of what those two horrible men might do to her mother. She then got up, cleared the scraps for her pet, put the dirty dishes in a bucket of water to soak, then rummaged in the refrigerator for the bag of bones they always kept for Lucy. The dog took the bone to the door, pushed it open with her nose and went outside.

Luke laughed. "Well, Babs it's like the blind leading the blind to watch the two of us limping around cleaning up the kitchen."

He soon went to the couch and groaned as he collapsed onto the cushions. Rubbing his knee, he finally relaxed; his head bobbed as Babs heard his breathing turn into soft snores.

CHAPTER TEN

Luke told the authorities if the crooks didn't drive the pickup with tender-loving-care, it would stall. Hawkman drove slowly, looking for a deserted truck, or any police action. He figured the vehicle would be found abandoned, and hopefully without containing the body of Annie Jones inside.

There were too many tracks, due to the authorities vehicles, to know which might have been made by Luke's truck. He needed to spot any traces of tire imprints that left the road and went into the forest.

Up ahead he saw police activity and stopped alongside the road. Standing on a small knoll overlooking a creek, Detective Chandler had his fists on his hips. Hawkman hopped out of his vehicle, and strolled to the top until he stood beside the detective. When he looked down, he saw why Chandler appeared so intense.

One of the police cars had a thick rope attached to the stout fender and slowly towed Luke's blue Ford pickup out of the shallow stream.

"Looks like the old engine couldn't take the strain," Hawkman said.

Chandler jerked his head around. "Good Lord, Casey, I'm losing it; didn't even hear you. Not good for me, that's for sure. You could have been a killer and I'd have been a sitting duck or already dead."

Hawkman smiled. "Don't worry, since you're still vertical, I won't tell anyone." He pointed toward the truck. "Anything inside?"

"No sign of the woman. However, we did find clues of her being in the pickup recently. Need to check with Luke and find out when she last rode in the vehicle, what clothing she had on when the men kidnapped her, and if she carried a hanky." He pulled a plastic bag from his pocket and showed him a white handkerchief with ragged embroidery on one edge.

"At least, it sounds like she's still alive," Hawkman said.

"No blood or evidence of a struggle. We did find three sets of footprints on the bank of the stream; like they were inside the pickup when they got stranded and had to climb out. We followed their tracks as far as we could before the ground became too grassy and the banks covered with rocks to tell which way they'd gone."

"Are you going to continue the search?" Hawkman asked, as he walked over to the pickup and put his hand on the hood.

Chandler nodded. "Yes, I'm shorthanded at this time, but we'll at least get a start. We have an idea of which direction they headed."

"Count me in."

"Thanks, follow me and I'll show you the footprints we found and how far they went."

Hawkman strolled along the yellow crime tape leading into the trees. He bent down a couple of times as he studied the prints.

"You can definitely tell the woman's shoes from the men's: much smaller and she's lighter weight."

"When I go back to Luke's house, I'm going to see if they have a picture of Mrs. Jones." Chandler said.

Hawkman stood. "If not, have Babs draw you a sketch. I have no idea what Annie looks like."

They came to the end of the tape, but due to Hawkman's training, he could see evidence of the trio traveling farther: broken branches, leaves knocked off the trees, grass that was still smashed down, and other tell tale signs. He stared toward the direction he figured the threesome had traveled.

"Casey, what's on your mind?" Chandler asked.

"I'm going to explore a bit. The hood on the truck felt warm, like it hasn't been too long since they deserted it."

"Be careful, those guys are armed and dangerous. I've got men coming who could accompany you."

"Can't wait. I don't want this trail to cool off. Tell them I'll mark my way with three rocks at the foot of trees about every five hundred feet or so."

"You got plenty of ammo?"

Hawkman nodded, as he pressed onward. "Pistol loaded with extra clip in my pocket."

Chandler watched Hawkman disappear into the shadows of the forest before he went back to his car. He flipped on the radio and yelled into the receiver. "Owens, where the hell are those men I told you to send up here?"

Owens radio squawked back. "They should be there by now."

"Haven't seen hide nor hair of them."

"Hold on, let me see if I can reach the men."

The detective eyed the road for several minutes before Owens came back on. "They're almost to the creek. Seems they took a wrong turn, but are on the right road now."

Chandler wiped a hand across his sweaty face. "Don't these new guys know how to read a map?"

"Yes, sir. You sound worried. Is something going down?"

"After finding the abandoned pickup, Casey didn't want to wait for me and the officers, so he took off alone to follow the clues the crooks left. The woman is with them and he wants to make sure she's safe. If he finds them, he'll need back-up. We need to be there."

About the time Detective Chandler decided to start out on his own to join Casey, a patrol car came bouncing onto the road near the creek. He waved at them to hurry up. The two hopped out and ran toward him.

"What's up?" one of the officers asked.

Chandler quickly explained as they headed toward the area where Hawkman had disappeared. Following the markers he'd left, the three men cautiously pursued the trail.

Thirty minutes passed before the detective held up a hand, put a finger to his lips, and drew his gun. He could hear muted voices coming from the area ahead. The men hunched down behind some brush and advanced slowly. Soon, through the branches they spotted Hawkman with his hands in the air, two men standing on each side of a woman with long blond hair; one had a gun trained on her and the other guy had his gun aimed at Hawkman. The female's hands were tied in front of her. She had her head bowed and appeared to be weeping.

Chandler recognized the two men as the bank robbers. One was about six foot tall and skinny; his greasy, dark brown hair was shoulder length, and his gaze darted from side to side. The other one stood about five foot six inches, had a crew cut, big ears, and a long hooked nose; reminded one of dumbo the elephant. They both wore dirty tee shirts, jeans and filthy tennis shoes.

Suddenly, the one with the crew cut raised his gun to the woman's chest. "You take one more step closer and she's dead meat."

"Let her go, and take me," Hawkman said, stopping in his tracks. "She's only slowing you down."

The tall man threw back his head and laughed. "She's our ticket to freedom; they want her back. You're just a cop. Your hide ain't worth a dime, so just shut up."

Crew cut grinned wickedly. "Hey, maybe we should take them both. Double ransom don't sound so bad."

"Naw, too much trouble to keep track of two. Let's just tie him to a tree and get on our way. Maybe his buddies will find him before he's devoured by a wild animal."

The tall guy, keeping his weapon trained on Hawkman muttered, "I'll tie him up; you make sure he doesn't do anything stupid. If he does, kill the woman." Taking a length of rope he had doubled in the loops of his jeans, he tied Hawkman to the nearest tree. He picked up the weapon from the ground, and stuck it in his pocket. "Okay, let's get the hell out of here."

The two rogues grabbed Annie's arms, her feet barely hitting the ground as they fled into the forest with her between them.

Chandler and his two officers bounded out of hiding.

"I'm afraid they're trigger happy and just might put a bullet into Annie," Hawkman said, as they untied him.

CHAPTER ELEVEN

Detective Chandler looked at Hawkman with surprise. "So what do you propose we do; not go after them? They've robbed a bank and kidnapped a woman. We need to catch these criminals."

"Too dangerous," Hawkman said, helping unwrap himself from the ropes. "Those two guys are really wired; it wouldn't take much to set them off. Our best bet is an ambush where we can grab Annie and get her to safety before seizing them."

"They could be many miles away before we find them again," Chandler said.

"I don't think so. As far as I could tell, they haven't slept or eaten. They're not going to have the energy to go far. I can track their trail."

"When?" the detective asked.

"We'll give them a head start; fool the idiots into thinking they've gotten away. Then we'll follow them quietly."

"Okay, but I'm not waiting much longer than thirty minutes."

"Fair enough. Do you have an extra gun I can borrow? They took mine."

***

Babs worried because no one had found her mother. She decided, since she knew the woods quite well, she and Lucy would take off and see if they could find her. Even though her ankle hadn't healed completely, she couldn't wait any longer. She'd rewrap the ankle, and would take just one crutch, which she could also use as a weapon if needed. The horrible men probably left the truck somewhere, as she knew it wouldn't go far without the loving touch of her dad.

Passing her sleeping father, she quietly went to her bedroom and dug out a couple of pocket knives she had stowed in her dresser drawers. She kept these honed to the sharpest, so if she had the urge to whittle, they were ready. This time their use might be for another purpose. She also grabbed a couple of long pins for securing her hair into a bun. They, too, might come in handy.

Babs snatched Lucy's leash off the hook on her bedroom wall; in case it got dark, she'd want her pet near her side. Rolling the long cord into a ball, she stuck it into her pocket, then softly closed the door. Her dad would think she remained in her room, and wouldn't know she'd left before morning.

She grabbed a small thermos that clipped onto her belt. When she got outside, she filled it with water from the well, rewrapped her ankle, rolled her long hair into a bun, stuck the pins in, then slipped one of the crutches under her arm, made a hand signal to Lucy, and away they went. She'd already made a plan in her mind where she would head first. There were caves near the creek, a perfect place to hide. However, you had to know where they were. She and Annie had discovered them on one of their exploring trips.

Her heart pounded when she thought of what her mom might be going through. A beautiful woman, and if these men so much as laid a hand on her, Babs would kill them.

Animal sounds had never frightened Babs, nor had the dark. She'd never been afraid of much of anything. Her dad had taught her how to track, kill pigs and skin deer for their smokehouse. She'd ran off a mountain lion and a bear by making them more scared of her than she of them. Respecting wild animals, she would let them have their territory until they invaded hers; then she figured they'd crossed the line.

With an overcast sky, Babs could smell rain on this warm day. Normally, a big storm skipped their area; a few sprinkles wouldn't hurt, as the land needed moisture, but a gully washer would wipe out clues.

It took almost an hour before Babs reached the creek. A path led up one side, and she spotted tracks that resembled those made by her Dad's truck, along with other recent tire treads. She followed them until she came to the spot where it appeared the pickup had tried to cross the small waterway and got stuck. Many crisscrossed ruts had been made in the ground recently. She stood back and tried to make sense of the muddy mess. Obviously, someone had pulled the truck out of the creek bed, and taken it away, as there were no markings on the opposite side.

Babs studied the ground around the area and spotted footprints leading into the trees. She bent down and examined them more closely. She swore in her mind that one set belonged to her Mother. Her excitement surged and she ran forward, following them until she reached the vegetation, which made it harder and she had to rely on other signs. Suddenly she came upon a tree with three small rocks stacked against its trunk. She scratched her head. It appeared someone had left clues; the kidnappers certainly wouldn't, so who?

Could the police have already found her Mother? No one had come to the house.

She continued on, following the signs and came upon several more rocks stacked in the same form. Then she discovered an area where it looked like a struggle had taken place; grass ripped up, branches broken. At that moment she spotted a piece of material hanging on a branch that looked like the same design as the blouse her mother had worn the morning those men took her. Babs caressed the cloth between her fingers, then stored it in her pocket. She also found rope pieces stuck on the tree trunk. Definitely, something had happened here.

Lucy followed Babs around the area. She suddenly stopped, sniffed the ground, and took off into the trees. Babs knew her dog didn't have any bloodhound in her, but the canine knew the scent of the family.

Babs quickly turned, and with the one crutch, hurried as fast as she could after her dog. Lucy kept circling back for her, then would take off again. Finally, Babs gave a few hand signals and the dog remained close, yet leading. She knew they were headed toward the caves hidden in the hills. These woods were fairly virgin and few people entered them, so she found it easy to follow the telltale signs of human activity.

The shadows were growing longer and the night would soon be upon them. It appeared she'd be spending the night outdoors. Sometimes the nights became quite cool and she hoped her jacket would be enough; if not, she'd cuddle with Lucy. Babs remembered a shallow cave which would be ideal for her and Lucy if they could get to it before darkness fell.

Babs had grabbed a handful of jerky before leaving home and filled the pocket of her jacket. Her Dad kept a supply on hand for snacks. She pulled a couple out and handed one to her pet, and they made their way, both chewing on their treat.

Soon they stood at the foot of the hill where the caves' openings were scattered across the front. Babs eyed the mouths of each one to see if she could see any movement. A couple were covered with brush and she couldn't examine the entrances. She remembered the first one appeared more shallow. Hidden by the bushes, she started up the side of the hill. She had to crawl and drag her crutch, trying to make as little noise as possible. Motioning for Lucy to stay beside her, she inched her way upward. Soon they were at the side and with enough light from the sun, she could see the inside of the cave which seemed clean of animal debris. Stepping on an extended rock ledge with her good foot, she swung herself into the opening. Lucy had no trouble jumping in beside her mistress. Babs leaned out the entrance and listened for any noise that might indicate her Mom and kidnappers were in one of the other caves.

***

Hawkman and the three police officers had no idea Babs and Lucy were about a quarter of a mile ahead. They trudged through the forest as Hawkman studied the trail to make sure he'd taken the right track.

"I don't know this part of the country real well, so I'm depending on the trail of clues the two men and Annie have left," Hawkman said, speaking softly.

"You're doing fine," Chandler said, following. "Just hope we can find them before dark."

"So where'd you take the pickup?"

"To the station lab so the tech guys could thoroughly go over it. When they're finished, we'll take it to Mr. Jones."

"Good, it's the only transportation he has. Before taking it to him, let Joe's Mechanic there in town check it over. I'll pay the bill."

"Will do. It could probably use a bit of tweaking, since it got stuck in the creek."

The men became silent as they continued on their trek through the woods.

CHAPTER TWELVE

Before Babs could draw her head back inside the cave, Lucy growled deep in her throat. Babs jerked around to see one of the men who'd kidnapped her mother standing at the edge of the cave with a gun pointed at her head. Her stomach felt like it had rocks in it. She quickly wrapped an arm around Lucy's neck to keep her pet from jumping the man and getting herself killed.

"My, my, who do we have here?" he said, with an evil grin.

Babs stared into his strange green eyes which darted around the cave, but would never gaze at her.

"Cat got your tongue." He laughed. "Guess not with a dog here."

She watched the gun in his hand. Strange he didn't have his finger on the trigger, but around the guard.

"So you're not going to talk. In that case, crawl out of there. You're coming with me."

Babs did as she was told and gave hand signals to Lucy, so she'd follow.

"What are you doing fooling around in the forest with a hurt ankle," he asked as they made it down to the floor of the hill.

She shrugged her shoulders.

"Don't you have a voice?"

She shook her head.

"You mute?" he asked.

Babs nodded.

"But you're not deaf?" he asked.

She again shook her head.

"I'll be damned, a mute who can hear. Never met a creature like you. Wait until I tell Howy."

He poked the gun into her back and pointed ahead. Lucy snarled at him. "Hey, call your dog off or I'll shoot her."

Babs gave a signal for Lucy to walk beside her.

"Smart dog. Just keep walking straight ahead; I'll tell you where to turn."

They went over rough terrain which made it hard for Babs on one crutch. They'd traveled to the end of the small mountain littered with caves. She felt extremely tired before he finally spoke.

"Okay, you can stop now."

He went over and moved a big piece of brush that looked like a gigantic tumble weed, then he pointed. "In here."

The sun had dropped quite a way in the sky, but still cast shafts of light so Babs could see inside the cavern. Howy sat on a large rock with a gun in his hand pointed toward the far wall.

"Glen, what the hell have you brought in? Food I hope."

"Not unless you're a cannibal, or like dog meat. I found these two roaming around and followed them to a cave at the end of the mountain. Didn't like them so close. Figured they're better off where we can keep an eye on them. There's an advantage here: this cute little gal is mute, so she won't be doing any screaming."

Suddenly, Lucy bounded toward the huddled figure on the far side. Whimpering, she nudged the person, until she stirred.

The woman turned over and looped her tied hands over Lucy. "I'm so glad to see you," she cried, tears running down her cheeks. Then she glanced over at Babs. "Oh my God, what are you doing here?"

Babs hurried to her mother and knelt down at her side. She wrapped her arms around the woman's slim shoulders and hugged her.

"Obviously, you two know each other," Glen said.

Annie glared at him. "Yes, this is my daughter. More than likely the police are right behind her."

Howy jerked around toward Glen. "Did you see anyone?"

"No, I figured it was just some kid out exploring."

"Howy stood. "You're a dope. Why would she be out climbing mountains with a crutch, unless she was looking for her mother?"

"Kids do crazy things. Maybe she was bored," Glen said.

"We gotta get moving. If the cops are behind her, we could be in big trouble," Howy said, pulling on a jacket. Then he stopped and had a funny grin on his face. "With two from the same family, we might be able to escape after all."

"If we don't get out of these hills soon, we'll both die of starvation," Glen said.

"Okay, ladies, let's get a move on it," Howy said, yanking Annie off the ground and pushing her toward the cave entrance.

"Leave my daughter here," Annie said. "She'll just slow you down with that bad ankle."

Howy raised an eyebrow, and gave Babs a shove. "Are you kidding. She got this far on it; she can travel just fine."

Lucy snarled at Howy.

"Hey, call that hound off."

Babs made some hand signals to Lucy, and she raced out of the cave.

"Where's she going?" Glen asked.

"To catch a rabbit," Annie said. "That'll keep her out of your hair for a while."

***

Hawkman hurried along, checking the clues as he led the three police officers through the forest. "I'm losing light under the shadows of the trees and it's getting harder to see where they've been."

"Maybe we should call it quits tonight and head out again first thing in the morning," Chandler said.

Hawkman leaned against the trunk of a large tree and looked down the darkened path. "As bad as I hate to call if off, we might have to. Otherwise, I might get us off on the wrong track, which would really waste precious time."

"In another thirty minutes it's going to be blacker than pitch in this forest," Chandler said. "We'd have to use our flashlights to continue."

"You're right, and that would give us away. Let's head back to the cars," Hawkman said.

They started back the way they'd come, when suddenly, a dog barking caught their attention. Hawkman swiveled around and Lucy came panting to him. "Lucy, what the hell are you doing out here?" Hawkman asked, as he bent down and patted the Labrador.

The canine turned and ran back the same direction she'd come, then ran back to Hawkman, barked and ran forward again.

"You know that dog?" Chandler asked.

"Yes, she's Babs' pet. She wants us to follow her. It must mean the girl's in trouble. This is the same way she acted when Babs fell, hurting her ankle."

"It must mean the girl's out there," the detective said.

"I'm afraid so. Lend me your flashlight, and you guys go ahead back to the cars," Hawkman said.

"We can't leave you in this situation. This girl could have found her mother and those robbers. She's no challenge to them. So, they've probably grabbed her too."

Hawkman raised his cowboy hat, and ran a hand over his hair. "I'm afraid that's what has happened. Babs directs the dog with hand signals, and she probably instructed her to go get help. The robbers would never know what she was doing."

Lucy whined, then grabbed Hawkman's jeans between her teeth and tried to drag him forward.

"We're going with you," the detective said. "This is going to be mighty interesting when the whole force ends up out here. We left our squawkers in the cars, but they can trace us through the GPS and since we haven't called in for several hours, they're going to get concerned."

"Thanks, Chandler, I appreciate it."

"Here's a flashlight; it's little, but has a big beam."

"Okay, Lucy, let's go," Hawkman said.

Lucy took off and the men followed in a trot.

CHAPTER THIRTEEN

Babs and Annie stepped out from the cave entrance into the dwindling sunlight. While the two men were talking off to the side, Babs, slipped a couple of pieces of jerky into her mother's hands, which she swiftly put into her mouth before the men joined them.

"Follow me," Howy said. "Glen, you bring up the rear."

They trudged through the high grass and were soon at a creek bank. Howy waded out into the water, splashed some onto his face and took a drink from his cupped hands. Annie and Babs hesitated.

Howy motioned for them. "Come on, it's shallow and the weather is plenty warm."

Babs knew it wasn't deep, but once they traveled in the water for any distance, Lucy would lose their scent. She walked on the side until Howy turned around and saw her.

"I said, get in the water," he growled. "You want me to throw you in? You're dog won't be able to find you, but she can go home."

Reluctantly, Babs tread into the creek. She hated getting her tennis shoes wet, but didn't want to cut her feet on the sharp bottom rocks or turn her ankle.

Annie, showing exhaustion, slipped several times and bruised her tied hands on the rough stones trying to catch herself. Babs planned to cut those ropes when she had the chance. She wondered why they hadn't tied her, probably because they figured a kid wouldn't give them a problem.

They journeyed a good quarter of a mile, before Howy finally climbed upon the bank and flopped down on the grass. Babs and Annie did the same, but stayed several feet from him. Before either man noticed, with one swift movement, Babs cut the rope around her mother's wrist and replaced the knife to her pocket.

Annie rubbed the places where the band had dug into her flesh, but didn't let the two men see her. She kept her hands together so they wouldn't know her arms were finally free of the binding cords.

"Thanks, sweetie, it's such a relief."

Babs nodded, as she stole a glance at the two criminals.

They rested for a few minutes before Howy stood. "Let's get rolling."

Unclipping the thermos from her jeans hoop, Babs took a swig of water and passed it to her Mom, who took it with both hands. After taking several gulps she handed it back to her daughter. Neither man saw them do this, as Glen had run up to Howy and pointed ahead at a shack on the side of the hill. Due to the dwindling day, Babs could barely see a thin curl of smoke emerging from the chimney.

Annie turned her head to see what they were looking at. "You know who lives up there, don't you?" she whispered to Babs.

The girl nodded.

Annie grinned. "They will be in for a big surprise if they try to approach Harmon. The hermit has probably already spotted our little tribe, and will be prepared."

Babs smiled as she remembered the first time she and Annie had met Harmon. They hadn't lived in these hills very long and were out exploring when they came upon the old log cabin. Not thinking anyone lived there, it surprised them when three huge howling bloodhounds, their long ears flopping in the breeze, came bounding and howling out from underneath the front porch.

Babs immediately threw herself over Lucy, covering her pet with her body, as three against one just wouldn't work. As suddenly as the dogs appeared, she heard a loud shrill whistle and the floppy eared dogs turned in their tracks and retreated. She and Annie peered up at the house where a tall, skinny man stood on the porch, looking like a giant. A long gray beard hung over bib overalls and a dingy white thermal top. Salt and pepper hair stuck out from underneath a straw hat perched on his head. Binoculars on a leather strap hung around his neck. Over his arm he carried a broken down double barreled shot gun. He walked to the edge of the porch and spit a stream of tobacco juice over the railing.

"What are you two doing so far away from home? You runnin' from the law?"

Annie laughed. "No, sir, my daughter and I decided to do a little exploring. We haven't lived here long and decided we should know a little about our surroundings."

"What's your names?"

"I'm Annie Jones and my daughter is Babs. She doesn't speak, but hears and understands everything you say."

"I know where you live. My name's Harmon, I'm a hermit who's lived in these hills for many years. Welcome."

"Thank you, Mr. Harmon," Annie said.

"No mister, just plain Harmon."

"We didn't mean to alarm you, Harmon. We'll be on our way." He nodded and walked back into his abode.

Babs' thoughts were interrupted by Howy's gruff voice. "Get a move on it. Someone's cooking up there in that shack and I'm mighty hungry."

Annie leaned toward Babs. "When he sees what Harmon's favorite meal is, he might think twice about wanting to eat. Speaking of food, do you have any more jerky?"

Babs slipped her mother another couple of pieces as they started trudging forward.

The distance to the cabin was much further than it appeared. When the party had reached the edge of the hermit's property, and the sun had almost dropped below the hills, three baying bloodhounds came running out from under the porch. Harmon sat in a wooden rocker, eyeing the four people coming toward his place; his shotgun across his lap. He stood and a shrill whistle stopped the dogs from attacking.

Howy had his pistol aimed at the first canine.

"Don't even think about shooting one of my dogs, or you'll be blasted by me." Harmon said, in a loud booming voice, his long gun drawing a bead on Howy. "Now, what do you people want?"

Howy gulped. "Food. We're hungry."

"I see," Harmon said. "How come you started out on a venture without carrying something to eat?"

Howy groped for words. "Uh, we ate it already. Didn't think we'd be gone this long."

"I don't believe you, but come in. Leave your weapons on the porch."

The two men dropped their guns on a bench. As Annie and Babs passed the hermit, he nodded.

Harmon watched them with an eagle eye as they paraded into his home.

Howy sniffed the air when they got inside the warm room. "Whatever you have cooking is making my stomach growl."

Harmon leaned his shotgun against the cabinet. "Have a seat, I'll dip you up some." He pulled out four metal bowls, moved the big pot to the center of the wood burning stove, then scooped up a hearty amount of stew into each.

Annie glanced at Babs and winked. Glen and Howy didn't seem to notice Annie no longer had the restraints on her wrists as she filled her large bent up spoon and put it to her lips, blowing on the hot food before putting it into her mouth.

Glen and Howy gobbled up their stew and Harmon filled their bowls again.

"Would you ladies like seconds? There's plenty here."

Annie and Babs shook their heads. "No, thank you, but it was delicious," Annie said.

She took her and Babs' empty bowls to the sink. Pumping water into the water basin, she soaked them, then waited for the men's and washed them all.

"Thank you," Harmon said.

Howy and Glen leaned back in the chairs and patted their full bellies. "Meat was really tender, and you had a group of vegetables I didn't recognize. Guess you do a lot of hunting in these hills," Glen said.

Harmon nodded. "Yep and I don't have to pay a dime for it."

"We thank you for your hospitality."

"You're more than welcome. Now I'd like to know why you have Annie and Babs Jones traveling with you?"

Howy's face fell. "You know them?"

"Sure do, they're my closest neighbors."

"Uh, they're our guides, showing us around," Howy said.

Harmon picked up his shotgun. "Sorry, but that's a lie. They'd never leave without carrying vittles into these wild areas."

"Speaking of food," Glen said. "What kind of animal made up the bulk of that soup?"

"Opossum," Harmon said.

Howy's and Glen's faces turned green. Glen jumped up from his seat, ran out the door where he leaned over the railing and retched. Annie covered her mouth to keep from giggling out loud.

When Glen came back inside, his face had turned gray and he sat back down next to Howy, holding his stomach.

"What's the matter with you two men? Have you never had opossum?" Harmon asked, the corners of his mouth twitching. "I'd like the answer to my question," as he lowered the shotgun until it was aimed at the two men's heads. "Annie and Babs, come over here and stand behind me. I don't want you hit by buckshot."

CHAPTER FOURTEEN

Hawkman and the clan of police officers jogged through the brush and trees following Babs' dog, Lucy. They paused at the creek where the canine ran back and forth, whining. A couple of times she jumped into the creek, but hopped back out.

Hawkman shined the beam of the flashlight up and down the bank where Lucy kept her nose to the ground. He could see many footprints in one area leading into the water; then up a few yards where Lucy seemed to be more focused, he saw only one set of prints.

Hawkman pointed the shaft of light onto the embankment. "It appears they went into the stream, but Babs stayed out until a few feet upstream. I imagine the guy leading the group figured the dog wouldn't be able to catch their scent if they traversed the middle of the brook."

"Wonder how far they'd go before climbing back on dry land?" Detective Chandler asked.

Hawkman rubbed his chin. "Hard to say. Let's follow the stream a bit, and Lucy will let us know."

They tramped up the side of the creek with Babs' pet leading the way. They'd traveled about a quarter of a mile when the dog let out a yip and headed inland at a run.

"Lucy, wait for us," Hawkman yelled.

The dog circled and barked at the men, then turned, scrambling ahead.

"She'll come back for us. It appears she's excited; Babs' scent must be strong."

***

Glen leaned over toward Howy, as if his stomach hurt, and whispered, "The cops are coming, I saw them. I've got our guns." He passed the weapon under the table. Howy discreetly slid it into his jeans pocket, and pulled his tee shirt down as he stood.

"I've got to get some fresh air," Howy said.

"Sit down. You still haven't answered why you have Annie and Babs traveling with you," Harmon said.

While Harmon had his attention on Howy, Glen aimed his gun from under the table in the hermit's direction and pulled the trigger.

Annie screamed as Harmon crumbled to the floor, holding his thigh, and dropping the shotgun. Howy grabbed it before Annie could get her hands on it. Not wanting to carry the bulky rifle, he unloaded it, tossed the shotgun and cartridges across the floor, pulled his pistol from his pocket, and pointed it at Babs and Annie.

"Let's get out of here."

"You can't leave this man bleeding on the floor; he might die," Annie said, her hands over her mouth.

"We have no choice. Get a move on," Glen said, giving the girls a shove toward the door. They jogged down the steps of the high porch and headed into the pitch black forest.

The bloodhounds didn't make any racket when the party left.

***

It had turned dark, and Harmon groaned, then felt the puddle of blood under his leg. He had to get the bleeding to stop, or he'd surely die on the floor of his house. He fished for his knife in his pocket, and ripped the leg of his overalls up to the crotch. It appeared the bullet had gone through the fleshy part of his leg, and had probably lodged in the wooden wall.

"Thank God, it didn't shatter the bone," he mumbled, searching for the small rope he always carried. Soon he found it on the loop on the side of his pants, and wrapped it around his leg above the wound, making a tourniquet. He felt light headed, but knew he couldn't afford to pass out. He needed some light so he could see how badly he'd been hurt.

Gritting his teeth and scooting on his butt, he made it to the small table beside the stove, where he remembered he'd placed the lantern. He always dropped a couple of matches beside it. After pumping it up, he lit it, adjusted the wick and placed it back on the table. The small room soon flooded with a dim light; at least he could examine his wound. It hurt worse than it looked. As he loosened the rope around his leg, he noticed the bleeding had almost stopped, so he tightened it again.

The bloodhounds started howling; then their tone changed to a friendly sound. Harmon heard the beat of a four-legged animal running up the stairs. His dogs were not allowed on the porch.

When the canine ran in the opened door, Harmon recognized her as Babs' pet.

"What in the world are you doing here, Lucy?"

The dog ran around him, sniffed at his leg and whined, then took off out the front.

He then heard the voices of men coming. Lucy ran in first and barked. Four men surrounded Harmon. A man with a patch over his eye and a cowboy hat bent over him, examined his leg, then stood.

"How are you doing? Are you in much pain?"

Harmon shook his head. "The pain has eased as long as I stay still."

We need to get you to a hospital. Looks like you've got the bleeding under control, but we have no idea how badly your leg is damaged."

The other three men were uniformed police, looking around the room.

"No sign of a phone. I'll step outside and see if I can by some chance get a cell phone signal," one of the officers said.

Hawkman turned his attention back to the injured man. "What's your name?"

"Harmon"

"Who did this to you?"

"One of the idiots who have Annie and Babs Jones as hostages. I fed them, but knew those two guys were scum. I took my eyes off of them for a second and one of them shot me; then they took off. Annie didn't want to leave, but they forced her."

"How long ago?' Hawkman asked.

"Couldn't have been over thirty minutes."

The officer on the porch poked his head inside. "I've been able to contact emergency. What's the longitude and latitude of this place? Also is there a flat area nearby big enough so a small helicopter can land?"

Harmon rattled off the longitude and latitude. "There's a flat place on the North side of the house."

Detective Chandler pointed at the shotgun on the floor. "Is this your weapon?"

"Yeah, one of those numbskulls pulled out the shells and tossed everything to the other side of the room. I'm surprised they didn't take it with them."

"Too cumbersome," Hawkman said.

The officer came in from the porch. "They're sending a medivac helicopter. Do you have more of those lanterns, so we can mark off the pad for the pilot?"

Harmon pointed to a small closet in the corner of the room. "You'll find three battery operated ones I keep for emergencies. They should work."

The officer grabbed them and motioned for the other two policemen to follow.

Chandler stepped over to Harmon. "Did you by any chance see what direction the group who shot you went?"

"No, I was on the floor when they took off."

The detective stepped over to the stove. "Better move this pot of food off the hot part of the stove; don't think you want it to burn the house down."

"Thanks. Have your men finish it off, if they like opossum."

Chandler grinned. "I love it. My grandma used to fix it for my grandpa; he got me to try it and I was hooked." He took a bowl out of the small cabinet and helped himself to a hearty portion. "How about you, Casey?"

"After we get Harmon on the helicopter, then I'll have some. Let your men eat first, I'm sure they're hungry."

Soon the chatter of the helicopter rotors were heard and it landed in the specified area. The officers directed the paramedics up to the house. They fastened Harmon into a gurney and took off within a matter of minutes. The bloodhounds howled, but never came out from underneath the house.

The men were all soon gathered back in the cabin. They put away the lanterns and gathered around the stove, Chandler explained what they were about to eat. Each man took a small bowl of the opossum stew. Once finished eating, they cleaned up their mess and turned to Detective Chandler.

"Not bad, never had opossum before," said one of the officers.

Hawkman walked outside. "Lucy, where are you?" He whistled, but didn't receive any response from the canine. He walked back inside. "Babs' pet has deserted us. She's probably back on her mistress' scent and took off."

CHAPTER FIFTEEN

Annie stopped and flopped down on a log, Babs followed suit. "We can't see squat; it's so dark. Why don't we just stop and try to get some sleep?"

"Easy for you to say; you're not being chased by the cops. Didn't you hear the helicopter earlier?" Glen asked, sitting down beside her.

"Yeah, but they fly over all the time. How do you know it was the police?"

"Just figured they're looking for us."

"Do you even know where you're going? We could be running in circles, " Annie said, rubbing her eyes.

The sky lit up with lightning; thunder rolled through the sky. "Looks like a storm is moving in," Howy said, standing in front of the three. "You live in this area; where are we?"

Annie sighed and pulled her jacket collar up. "I'm never out at this time of night. I couldn't see any landmarks in this darkness, even if they were right in front of me. The sky is overcast, there's no moon, and it's getting cold."

Glen stood. "We need to find some sort of shelter or we're going to get soaking wet."

"Good luck. This is a very desolate area. Harmon's shack is the only one I know of."

A noise behind Babs made her jerk her head around. Lucy jumped over the log and practically landed in her lap, so excited to find her mistress.

Glen jumped back and pulled his gun.

"No!" Annie screamed. "It's just Lucy."

"How'd that damn dog find us again?" Glen asked, pocketing his gun.

"You don't separate Lucy from Babs," Annie said.

"I thought it might be a mountain lion."

"Wild animals sense a storm and find shelter. You won't need to worry about them tonight. However, we need to think about us finding refuge before this storm hits."

"Any suggestions?" Howy asked.

"The caves, but I'm so turned around, I have no idea which direction to go," Annie said, throwing her hands in the air. "We could try to find a stand of trees with the tops intermingled; it would keep off some of the rain. However, if there's strong wind, it wouldn't help."

Howy motioned to the group. "Let's keep moving. Maybe we'll find some sort of cover."

The wind howled as it made its way through the branches, throwing leaves and twigs every which way. Lightning flashed and thunder roared, then the rain came down in torrents. Fighting their way through the forest, Annie and Babs didn't even consider being hostages at this time; they just wanted to get out of the way of the storm's wrath.

They were all soaked to the bone, when the sky lit up. Howy yelled over the noise. "Up ahead, I see a building."

Everyone quickened their step toward the small shed. Annie, Babs, and Lucy stood back and huddled together as the two men worked on the padlock securing the door. Finally, the two men stepped back as Glen shot off the lock. With the thunder and rain noise, no one worried about the sound attracting any attention.

They all scurried inside, brushing spider webs out of their faces, and when Lucy shook, she sprayed them all with water; then they waited for a burst of illumination so they could tell what they'd entered. When it finally came, Annie noticed a chain hanging from the ceiling. She reached up, pulled it; light flooded the room.

"Who would have dreamed this place had electricity," Howy said, scratching his head.

Annie's and Babs' gazes examined the room. It contained three small cots with blankets, pillows and a campers stove along with shelves holding dry and canned food stuffs. Babs opened a small cabinet where she found more canned goods, metal plates, utensils, couple of can openers, towels, and washcloths.

"This looks like a hunter's shack," Annie said. "Obviously, someone with money to have electricity wired to it."

Annie grabbed a large pan and took it to the door.

"What are you doing?" Glen asked.

"I'm going to catch some rain water."

"Good idea."

Babs went to the cabinet and picked out a can of Vienna Sausages, opened them and put them in a plate for Lucy.

"Hey, don't feed the dog the good stuff," Howy growled.

Babs pointed to the shelf which contained at least ten cans of the same item. Howy's face turned red, but he remained silent. When Annie returned, she rubbed her arms.

"It's cold out there. I'm happy we found this place," she said, examining other things in the room. Hidden behind a long sheet were jackets, jeans and shirts. She looked them over for hidden spiders, then held them up to her body.

"You guys look the other way, I'm getting out of these soaked clothes."

Babs went to her side and held the drape in front of her mother as she changed. Then Annie handed her daughter a set of clothes.

"Try these; I think they'll fit you."

Babs scooted behind the cover.

"Anything in there suitable for us?" Glen asked.

Annie rolled her eyes. "I'm not your mother. You'll have to come and look for yourself."

Soon they were all in dry clothes. Hanging their wet garments around the room on hangers and nails driven in the walls, Annie watched them drip water onto the wooden floor and shook her head. "They'll never dry with all this humidity. So we'll have to leave them for whoever owns this place."

"Do you think the owners will come soon?" Glen asked.

"I doubt it; nothing is in season right now, except fishing. They probably won't be here before fall," Annie said. "Anyway, no one would be hunting in this storm."

"That's a relief."

Annie yawned. "I'm going to lie down and get some rest." She and Babs checked the cots and shook out the covers, then climbed in.

"I'm not sleepy yet," Howy said, "I'll take the first watch."

"Okay," Glen said, and reclined on the camp bed.

***

Hawkman sat across from the detective at Harmon's kitchen table. "Looks like a storm is moving in. I won't be able to track them; and without Lucy, it appears hopeless."

"Let's get back to our vehicles. I'll see about getting a helicopter. This following them on foot is hell in these hills."

"I agree. We better get a move on it. We'll probably get drenched before we make it back as it is. I'll go by the hospital and see Harmon, if it's not too late."

"Do we need to feed his dogs?" Chandler asked.

"No, they're hunting dogs, they'll find their own meals."

A clap of thunder shook the shack and the dogs howled.

"Let's get going; the storm sounds like it's right on top of us," the detective said.

The men turned out the lanterns, clamored out of the house, locked the door and headed in a trot back into the woods toward where they'd left their vehicles. They didn't make it halfway before the rain came down in torrents. All four of the men were soaked by the time they came in sight of their cars.

Since they were so close to Luke Jones' place, the officers and Hawkman drove down to see him before heading for town. They stood outside the front door instead of going inside with their dripping wet clothes.

Luke stood with his head bowed as he heard the tale of his daughter and wife. "I knew Babs had gone to find her mother when I finally went into her room and found she hadn't slept in her bed. You're sure they're okay?"

"Yes," Hawkman said. "They just keep slipping out of our reach. When the storm passes through, we'll get a helicopter in there; it'll be much easier to spot them. Those men won't hurt the women as long as they need them."

"Thank you for all you're doing." Luke raised a hand. "Oh, could they fix my truck?"

"I'm sure they were able to repair it. I'll check when I get into town and have someone bring it out, probably tomorrow." Hawkman assured him.

Luke nodded, turned back into the house and flopped down on the couch.

CHAPTER SIXTEEN

Hawkman turned toward Chandler before stepping off Luke's covered front porch into the rain. "I'm going to swing by home and change into some dry clothes. I'll stop by the station after I pay a visit to Harmon."

Chandler waved and dashed to the patrol car. Hawkman took it slow on the dirt road, where the ruts had already filled with water and slipping off into the ditch would not be fun. He soon arrived home and Jennifer met him at the door. She immediately sent him to the laundry room, but followed him, asking questions as they went.

Miss Marple tagged along behind them into the washroom; and when Hawkman removed his mud clad boots, she hissed and jumped out of the way as he placed the dirty footwear on the floor beside her.

"Stinky boots," Jennifer said, picking up the smelly pair and placing them in the sink.

Hawkman filled her in while undressing; then naked, he sprinted for the bedroom to shower. "Could you fix me a sandwich while I'm scrubbing off the grime?" he called over his shoulder.

"Okay."

He soon returned to the kitchen and sat down at the bar. "This looks wonderful," he said, eyeing the Dagwood sandwich Jennifer had prepared. "I definitely need refueling."

Jennifer sat down opposite him. "So, no sign of Babs and Annie?"

"There were signs, but they tended to stay just a step ahead of us; then this storm hit, Lucy took off and didn't return, so it all went down the tubes. I'm going back to town and see if Harmon's okay. Not sure if they'll be keeping him overnight or not. If he needs a ride back home, I'll probably take him, so don't expect me back any time soon."

"How's Luke taking all this?" she asked.

Hawkman took a deep breath and exhaled. "He's depressed. His knee won't let him help us in the search for the two women he loves, and he has no way to communicate: no phone and his truck is in the shop."

"My gosh, you'd think he'd at least have a phone. Maybe we should get him a cell phone."

"I don't think it would work, as he's down in that valley and you know how hard it is for us to get a call through on ours; no towers nearby to give a good signal. A landline would be his best bet, but he doesn't have any money to get one installed. I'm hoping his truck will be fixed by tomorrow."

He finished his food and picked up the extra set of clothes he'd placed on the counter. "Just in case I get wet again. It's not comfortable running around in soggy jeans. Think I'll keep an extra set in the 4X4; I never know when I might need them."

Jennifer glanced out the kitchen window. "It's still gloomy, but it appears the worst of the storm has passed." She walked him to the door and gave him a kiss. "Be careful."

He grinned. "My middle name."

On his way to the Medford Hospital, Hawkman thought about Harmon's wound, and figured the man would want to leave all the staff's attention when he could. It didn't appear a terrible injury and he'd probably be able to recover at home with a handful of antibiotics.

Hawkman soon drove into the emergency parking lot, found an empty slot and headed for the door. He explained to the receptionist that Harmon was brought in by helicopter with a gunshot wound to his leg.

"Are you a relative?" she asked.

"No. I'm Tom Casey, Private Investigator." He pulled out his badge. "I'm here to take him home, if the doctor releases him this evening."

The woman pulled a report out of the files on the desk. Hawkman sneaked a peek and learned Harmon's last name was Getty.

"He's out of surgery, so if you'll have a seat, I'll check with the doctor."

Hawkman strolled over to a chair near the desk and sat down. Within a few minutes, the woman returned.

"Mr. Casey, if you'll follow me, I'll take you to Mr. Getty."

They walked down the hallway to a small room, where Harmon reclined with his eyes closed. He quickly opened them when he heard the woman's voice telling Hawkman to go right in.

"Man, I'm glad to see you," Harmon said. "I hope the storm has passed so you can take me home."

"Did the doctor release you?"

"He said I could go home tonight."

"Okay, let me go check about the paperwork with the front desk and we'll get you out of here."

It didn't take long before Hawkman had Harmon tucked into the SUV, and they were on the road.

"I'll need instructions on how to get to your place, even though I've been there; we were on foot."

Harmon quickly told him.

Hawkman nodded. "Got it. You feel like talking? I need to ask you some questions."

"Sure. Did you guys catch the robbers?"

"No, unfortunately, Babs' dog, Lucy, took off just as the big storm rolled in. We weren't able to follow. Thank goodness, we got you to the hospital."

"I appreciate it, too. About thirty minutes after I got here, the thunder rolled across the sky and the rain came down in buckets."

"What I need to know is about the area behind your place. Are there any homes or buildings where criminals could take cover?"

Harmon scratched his beard. "No full time residents that I know about. It's rugged country. About the only thing I can think of are a few shacks where hunters can get out of the weather, or even spend the night. They're usually supplied with a few rations, extra clothes and couple of cots. One or two have strung wires to the few scattered electric poles, and have run power to these little houses. Guess they figured the utilities companies wouldn't notice."

"How did you find out about these places?"

"I hunt a big swatch of those woods and have come across two of those little shacks, and I'm sure there are more."

"How far is the nearest one to your place?" Hawkman asked.

Harmon looked up at the ceiling of the vehicle in thought. "I'd say five or six miles straight behind my house. The other one I spotted was due east about eight miles."

"You walk that far?"

"Yep."

"What kind of game do you take home?"

"Anything from rabbit and deer to bears. I've got a smokehouse, and tan the hides, so nothing goes to waste."

"You're definitely self-sufficient."

Harmon grinned through his scraggy beard. "A man and his dogs gotta eat."

"How come you don't have electricity?"

"No income."

Hawkman laughed. "Makes sense. I did notice you have a pump at your sink."

"I found an underground stream right next to my place. Went to the dump, found some pipe and ran the water to the house. Don't have much pressure, but it works for what I need."

"How'd you get to the dump? I didn't see any vehicle at your place."

"Well, it's an all day affair. On the side of the house is a lean-to with a bedding area for Jake my mule. I hitch a wagon to him early in the morning and we slowly make it to town, do the errands and return home just before dark."

"Looks like your life out here in the boonies is very pleasant and laid back."

Harmon nodded. "I like it."

Darkness had fallen as they arrived at Harmon's place. The dogs howled and ran around happily greeting their master.

"Take it easy, boys, don't need you jumping on my sore leg."

Hawkman offered his arm, but Harmon refused it as he limped to the front and climbed the stairs to the porch.

"Thank you, for bringing me home. Feel free to bring the police to search these hills through my place."

"You'll probably hear a helicopter coming over tomorrow. I think that will be our best bet."

Harmon waved as he disappeared into his cabin.

CHAPTER SEVENTEEN

Once the bloodhounds realized their master had returned home, they stopped howling and settled under the porch. Hawkman turned around and drove out the way he'd come.

After pulling into his garage, he noticed the dashboard clock read midnight. Jennifer had left the small kitchen light on, so when he stepped inside, he immediately found a note on the counter. Detective Chandler wanted him to call regardless of the time. He'd arranged for a helicopter and they needed to be at the pad by six o'clock in the morning.

Hawkman picked up the landline and poked in the digits. Chandler answered in a sleepy voice and told him they had the copter. Did he want to go on the search? Hawkman verified he did and would meet them at the pad.

After hanging up, he dialed the automatic coffee maker to start at four, then quietly went to bed in hopes of not waking Jennifer. She moaned and rolled over when he climbed in beside her, but didn't awaken.

Wednesday morning, he got up at four-thirty, dressed, filled a thermos full of coffee and grabbed a yogurt from the refrigerator. He wrote a quick note to his wife before heading for the garage. The sun had not peeked over the mountains yet, and the cool crisp air cleared his brain of cobwebs as he climbed into the 4X4. He had plenty of time to get to Yreka, so he drove slowly to avoid being startled by a deer jumping onto the road. The weather hadn't really heated up yet, and he really enjoyed this time of year.

Hawkman soon rolled into town and drove straight to the pad on the outskirts of the city. He had about fifteen minutes to kill. The helicopter had just landed, and its rotors were winding down. Detective Chandler hadn't arrived, so he sat in his vehicle sipping coffee and watching the maintenance men check over the machine. When the pilot climbed out of the aircraft, he removed his helmet. He appeared close to six feet tall, and wore the traditional pilot flight gear.

Within a few minutes, Chandler drove up with Officer Owens. Hawkman hopped out of his 4x4 and walked over to the unmarked car. The Detective had a cup of coffee in his hand, and rolled down his window.

"Beautiful day we have working for us. Want a cup of java?" Chandler asked.

"No, thanks, brought a thermos with me. I talked with Harmon last night."

The detective took a swig of coffee. "Oh, yeah. How's he doing?"

"Good. I took him home and he told me about these hunter shacks scattered throughout the forest. He told me the location of a couple. I think we should check them first."

Chandler nodded. "I've heard they could have extra clothes, rations and even cots. Ideal for our armed gang." He climbed out of the car. "Let's go talk with the pilot. He's familiar with this area. Once you tell him where these buildings are, he'll probably be able to pinpoint the exact spot."

The three men sauntered over a short span of newly mowed grass to the helicopter pad. The pilot, with his flight helmet nestled under his arm, turned toward them, and held out his hand to Chandler.

He grinned. "Good morning, detective. You awake yet?"

Chandler shook his head. "Barely." He turned to Hawkman. "Dan Wren, meet Private Investigator Tom Casey. He'll be joining us."

"Welcome aboard," he said, shaking Hawkman's hand.

Hawkman observed the man's sharp green eyes, nose with a bump as if it'd been broken, and neatly cropped brown hair. When Dan smiled, Hawkman noticed his teeth were slightly crooked, but hidden by a lopsided grin and a trimmed mustache. He guessed he'd be in his late thirties or early forties

The men climbed aboard the aircraft, and buckled their seat belts. Before starting the rotors, Dan turned in his seat.

"My understanding is we're looking for a couple of robbers with two women as hostages. Do you have some idea of which direction they're traveling?"

Hawkman remembered Harmon's instructions when the Medical helicopter came, so he rattled off the latitude and longitude of Harmon's place. "Five or six miles straight behind his house there's a hunter's shack, and another one is approximately eight miles due east. I thought those might be a good couple of places to start the search."

Wren was jotting notes, then glanced at Hawkman. "I'm familiar with those hunter rest cabins. An ingenious idea for those guys who walk for miles to hunt, but don't want to go into town at night to rent a motel. These small out buildings are fairly easy to spot from the air."

***

Annie awoke to Lucy's whining and glanced at the dog. She had her paw on Babs' leg trying to get her attention. The animal needed to go outside, but no way could Annie let her out without waking Howy. He'd scooted the cot in front of the door, and Glen was asleep sitting up, but leaning against the wall. So she decided to forget about keeping these two happy and yelled.

"Lucy needs to go outside. If you don't let her out, she'll pee on the floor or worse."

Howy lurched straight up, and waved his gun in the air. "What's going on? Why are you yelling, woman?"

"Let the dog out so she can go pee," Annie said. "Let me out, too."

"Only one of you at a time," Glen said, rubbing his eyes.

She frowned at him in disgust. "Have you lost your mind? You think for one minute I'd run off with my daughter in here with you two lugs? So move out of the way before I wet my pants."

Howy narrowed his eyes and pointed the gun at Annie. "You ain't the boss, lady."

"I don't aim to be, but at least let the dog out; I'll just go over here in the corner."

Howy stood up and shoved the cot out of the way. "Go. If you aren't back within five minutes, I'll be out to get you."

"Fair enough," Annie said, hurrying out the door.

Babs lay on her stomach, arm crooked with her chin resting on the palm of her hand as she listened to the discussion between Annie and the two men. It made her proud to hear her mom so fearless.

She soon turned over, swung her legs off the cot and stood. The little window let in the morning sunshine, which provided enough light to see where she stepped without tripping.

"Where do you think you're going?" Glen asked, lowering his pistol and pointing it at Babs' heart.

She motioned to the cabinets, rubbed her stomach and pretended to eat.

"I'm hungry too," he said getting up, sliding the pistol into the waist of his jeans.

He stepped beside her as she removed several cans of sardines, Vienna Sausages, Spam and various potted meats she didn't recognize. Glen picked up the box of crackers she'd placed on the counter.

"Wonder how stale these are?" he asked, then slammed them down on the surface.

Babs gave him a disgusted look and shrugged her shoulders. She then turned around when she heard the scratching on the door. Howy opened it a couple of inches, then let Lucy and Annie inside. Annie carried the pan of caught rainwater and set it on the floor. Joining Babs at the cabinets, she picked out a couple of the cans of sardines, tossed them onto the cot, along with the box of crackers, then opened a can of the sausages for Lucy. She also grabbed a small pan and dipped it half full of water for the dog.

After eating, Annie went to the small closet where she'd seen a backpack, took it to the cabinet and loaded it with food that could be eaten on the trail.

Glen watched her. "Is there another pack?"

"Yes, it's bigger. I'd advise you guys to load it up, as this one is just for me, Babs and Lucy."

"Oh yeah, who says?" Glen snarled.

"I do, because I can't carry anything heavier, and I don't want you yelling at me to hurry."

"She's got a point," Howy said, as he went over and grabbed the big pack.

Before they finished unloading the cabinet, Glen put his finger to his lips. "Quiet, I hear a helicopter."

Babs ran to the small window, only to have Glen grab her and shove her to the floor. "Don't go near the window. They probably have high powered binoculars and would notice any movement."

CHAPTER EIGHTEEN

Once the men were seated in the helicopter, the aircraft lifted and soared just above the treetops. Hawkman put the binoculars to his eyes.

Dan Wren, the pilot pointed. "Just ahead to our right I see the top of a small building."

Hawkman and Chandler shifted their heads and studied the area.

"It certainly looks like what Harmon described as a hunter's shack," Hawkman said.

"Do you see any signs of human invasion?" Chandler asked.

"Nothing. Swing around to the East and let's check the other one. Keep your eyes open for sheds, as Harmon figures they're scattered through the region."

The copter made a sharp turn and headed east. Within a few minutes, Wren motioned.
"There it is."

Hawkman studied the structure. "Looks identical to the other one. Wonder if they belong to the same person?"

"Could be a hunting club," Chandler said.

"I want to check something. Would you mind circling back to the first one?"

"Sure, no problem."

"Check the door, if possible." Hawkman said. "See if there's a chain and padlock on it."

The men had their binoculars to their faces as they rotated around the small building.

"Yeah, there's a chain with a padlock." Owens said. "The chain is looped around the handle, and the lock is hanging from a link, but it's not locked."

"Yep, I see it too," Chandler said.

"Appears someone has broken into it," Hawkman said. "Is there any place nearby you can set this craft down?"

Wren shook his head. "Forest is too dense here. I did see a place big enough to set down next to the cabin we flew over."

"That was Harmon's place. A medical helicopter landed there, and took him to the hospital," Hawkman said. "It's about five miles from the hunter's shack. I think we should land and check them."

***

Howy and Glen cleaned out the small pantry of food stuffs.

"This should hold us for several days. Surely we'll be out of these mountains by then," Howy said.

Glen cocked his head, and put a finger to his lips. "Listen. I hear a helicopter again."

"We better get out of here when they leave. I think they've gotten wise," Howy said, throwing the backpack over his shoulders.

Babs tightened the bandage around her ankle, which she thought would never dry after their trek through the creek. She decided not to mess with the crutch any more; it had begun to get in her way, so she stood it in the corner. Taking the water bottle from the hook on her jeans, she filled it with water from the pan.

"What are you doing?" Glen asked.

Babs held up the bottle.

"Give it to me," he said.

She shook her head, and he grabbed at it, but she put it behind her. He took hold of her long hair and yanked her toward him, then slapped her hard across the face. Lucy snarled and lunged at him. Glen fell backwards and pulled his gun.

"No!" Annie screamed, as she dove for the dog.

"Call that damn animal off or I'll shoot her."

Babs quickly signaled for Lucy to back off, while she rubbed her cheek with her other hand.

"Everyone shut-up," Howy yelled. "With all this commotion, they're bound to hear you over the rotors on the helicopter. Glen, you'd be a fool to fire your gun at this point. Let's just get the hell out of here, before they come back with a swat team." Howy listened and when he could no longer hear the rotors, he opened the door and looked around. "Okay, the coast is clear, move it, move it," he said, shoving Annie and Babs outside.

They fled the little shack and hightailed it into the wooded area with Howy leading the pack and Glen bringing up the rear.

Babs noticed the heavy backpack of food caused Annie to tire faster. When they stopped for a quick rest, Babs took a few of the cans out and placed them in her pockets, hoping to lighten her mother's load. Her hand rubbed against the two pocket knives she'd forgotten about; they still might come in handy. The hooded sweatshirt she'd nabbed from the closet at the shack had bigger pockets and was warmer than the one she'd left behind. They were soon on their way with Lucy never leaving Babs' side. When Glen got near her, Lucy bared her teeth and growled deep in her throat. It indicated to Babs her pet would die for her, so she kept her close.

Howy dropped back so he padded along beside Annie. "You live in these hills, tell me how long before we get out of them?"

Annie glanced up at the angle of the sun. "We're going due north, which means we're going deeper into the forest. If we keep going in this direction, it will be a long time before we get out." She pointed. "We'll have to crest those mountains."

He rubbed the back of his neck. "That's a hell of a long hike."

She shrugged. "It all depends on how far you want to go to get away from the law. Also, if you decide to continue this way, I'd suggest you save your ammunition, as there are wild animals such as bears, cougars and poisonous snakes in those hills; much more dangerous than me, Babs, or Lucy."

He scratched the stubble on his chin. "Which way would be the shortest way out of here?"

She pointed behind her. "South, the way we came."

"You wouldn't lie to me would ya?"

"Of course, I'd like to go home, but I'm telling you the truth. Your sight should tell you." She waved a hand skyward. "Just look over this rugged country. There's not so much as a path as far as the eye can see."

Howy took off his camouflaged cap and wiped his forehead on the crook of his arm, then flopped the hat back on his head. "You two stay right here, I've got to speak to Glen in private."

Annie took off the backpack and rested it against the fallen log where she and Babs sat. Lucy lay at their feet, and snacked on a can of meat Babs opened for her.

"I don't think these guys are as tough as they'd like us to believe," Annie whispered. "When Glen slapped you, he just wanted to show you who's boss. I know it stung like hell, and he deserved a kick in the butt. Knowing he had a gun, I didn't dare jump him, afraid he might use it. However, I don't think he'll try it again."

Babs grinned, patted her mom's arm, then gave Lucy a rub on her head.

Howy and Glen strolled toward the two females. Glen stepped in front and smirked at Annie. Lucy bared her teeth and growled.

"Shut-up, dog." Then he gave Annie his attention. "Are you pitching a line to my partner here, telling him if we keep heading north we won't run into anything but wild animals?"

"Look for yourself," Annie said, standing. "You've got eyes. Do you see cabins, roads, or high wires of any sort? This is wilderness."

"So to get out of here we'll need to head south? How about southwest or southeast?"

Annie raised her hands. "Any of those directions will get you back to civilization."

"Do you know where we are now?" Glen asked.

"No, I've never been this far north."

"Then how do you know there are no living beings ahead?"

Annie put her hand on her hips. "You guys sure didn't do much planning for your escape after you robbed the bank; if you don't even have a destination. I would have thought you'd have it all mapped out."

Glen glared at her. "We don't need a lecture from you. Just tell me how you know so much."

Annie exhaled loudly. "Not only do I live in this area, I've talked with men who hunt these hills and they told me how desolate it is. That's why those little shacks are scattered around. They built them so they'd have protection from the elements. I'm not sure if there are any past this point, as it would take pack mules to bring in the lumber, and they sure wouldn't have electricity."

"What about water?" Howy asked.

"There's streams all over, but I couldn't tell you where they are this far north."

Glen glanced toward Babs. "Gather your gear and let's get moving. We'll need to find a place to camp before dark."

CHAPTER NINETEEN

Wren brought the helicopter down for a soft landing on the clearing next to Harmon's place, and cut the rotors. The four men climbed out and hopped to the ground. Hawkman tugged the backpack, full of sandwiches and bottled water, over his shoulders, then they all walked the few yards to the front of the cabin. The bloodhounds howled, and Harmon, his shotgun cradled over his arm, stood on the porch staring at the group.

Hawkman yelled up at him, "Hey, Harmon, Tom Casey here." He pointed toward the aircraft. "Is it all right if we leave the copter there?"

Harmon whistled at the dogs to silence them. "No problem. You obviously haven't found those rowdies who kidnapped Annie and Babs."

Hawkman shook his head as he stood with legs spraddled and fists on hips. "Nope, they're keeping one step ahead of us. We want to check out the hunter's shack behind your place."

"I'd like to go with you, but don't think I'm ready to do much walking yet."

"No problem. You get healed so you can do more hunting," Hawkman said. "By the way, would you mind if our pilot, Dan Wren, joined you on the porch?"

"Not at all, I'd like some company."

Hawkman motioned for the pilot to grab a couple of sandwiches and drinks from the pack. The dogs made grunting noises as Dan warily climbed the wooden steps.

"Pay no attention to those hounds. They make lots of noise, but they're harmless," Harmon said.

"We'll be back before dark," Hawkman called, as he, Chandler and Owens trooped toward the back of the house and headed north.

As the men moved deeper into the forest, the undergrowth and fallen logs kept them at a slow pace, but trying to go any faster could cause a fall or injury. Hawkman had clipped a small compass onto one of his jeans' belt loops so they could keep on track in case it became overcast.

As the sun climbed higher, the humidity inside the tree laden area caused the sweat to soak through the men's shirts and the flying bugs to swarm their faces. Soon, Hawkman spotted the hunter's shack and put up a hand. They progressed with caution, not knowing if they'd find the group inside. Hawkman pulled his gun and hunkered down as he advanced toward the door. The two officers followed his lead. They lined up alongside the building, backs against the wood siding with weapons poised. Hawkman pushed open the door with his foot.

When they received no action, Hawkman peeked around the jamb. The shack was empty. He holstered his Beretta and waved the other men inside.

Hawkman put his thumbs in his jeans' back pockets and glanced around. "They've been here. These look like women's damp clothes hanging on these nails and backs of chairs." He held up a damp sweatshirt. "This looks like one I've seen on

Babs. They must have gotten soaked yesterday in the downpour." He examined the other garments. "The rest are men's pants and shirts."

Detective Chandler stood in front of a small closet. He held back the sheet covering the opening. "Looks like this is where they found extra clothing. There are empty hangers and a couple of shirts still here."

Hawkman stepped toward the open cabinet doors, and accidentally kicked a metal plate. He bent over and picked it up, plus an empty can of Vienna Sausages. "Looks like Lucy is with them."

"They've practically emptied all the food stuffs." Officer Owens said, holding up a small can. "All except for the liver. I can see the dust rings, and it appears these cabinets were loaded."

The detective frowned. "They must have found some sort of packs or bags, otherwise, how else could they carry it all?"

Hawkman nodded. "Makes sense. Hunters might well need packs to carry equipment, ammunition, and such while in the field. They probably stored some extras."

Chandler pointed at the rumpled covers on the beds. "These cots have been slept in too."

"I think we can definitely come to the conclusion they've been in this shack." Hawkman said.

"No doubt," Owens and Chandler echoed.

"I wonder how much of a start they have on us?" Chandler asked.

"Probably not more than a couple of hours." Hawkman opened the door leading outside. "Let's see if we can find their tracks."

The three men trouped out of the building, and immediately spotted footprints leading north in the water-soaked soil. The trail stayed visible until they got into the heavily vegetated area, then it all but disappeared. Hawkman would have to depend on his tracking skills.

Near a big fallen branch, Hawkman pointed out to the two officers an empty can of a meat product lying on the ground. "Since there's only one can, appears they stopped and fed Lucy." He picked it up and examined the inside. "It hasn't been here long, no insects have found the residue yet."

They continued on, reassured when they found foot and dog prints, indicating they were still behind their quarry. During the trek, they discovered several sheltered areas with food cans scattered across the ground.

The detective sat down in the shade on a fallen log. "Got to take a break. How about one of those sandwiches?"

Hawkman felt relieved of the strain on his back when he shed the backpack and rested it against the huge tree trunk. The men ate in silence for a few minutes, then Hawkman looked out over the territory and glanced at the compass hanging at his side. "They're going due north, and there's nothing ahead but wilderness. Do these guys have a plan or are they just running?"

"Neither of them are from this part of the country, so I doubt they know beans about where they're going." Owens said.

"Not smart to hightail it through unchartered territory," Hawkman said.

Chandler glanced up and harrumphed. "Haven't met a bank robber yet that had any sense."

Hawkman smiled. "You're right. They wouldn't be criminals if they had a brain."

"Wouldn't Annie and Babs know where they were?" Owens said.

Hawkman pulled the pack over his shoulders. "It's possible, but we're a long way from their home. Not sure they've hiked this far on an excursion. These guys might feel it below them to ask a woman where they are."

Owens nodded. "I hear ya."

Chandler groaned as he got to his feet. "I've never walked so much in my life. My body will pay for it tomorrow." He glanced at his watch. "We better get going. It's noon and we'll only be able to go a couple more hours, if we plan to get back to Harmon's before dark."

They trooped on north for a mile or so and Hawkman raised a hand, then pointed to ground. "Look at this mashed grass." He studied the area ahead and noticed some broken small limbs. A sunbeam hit something on the ground, sending a flash of light into his face. He hurried forward and found a full can of a meat product. It had either fallen out of a pack or dropped on purpose. "Looks like they've changed directions."

"We may be gaining on them, so keep voices low, eyes peeled and noise to a minimum." Chandler said.

They moved along at a steady pace in single file, watching for the subtle clues along the way. Due to the humid heat, even though cool breezes prevailed when you got out into the open areas, sweat ran down Hawkman's face and he was constantly wiping it away with his sleeve. He could feel the trickles running down his back and sides, plastering his clothes to his body.

Jerking up his head, he quickly ducked behind a large redwood tree. The detective and Owens followed his lead.

CHAPTER TWENTY

"Did you see something?" Chandler whispered, his gun drawn.

"No. I heard a dog bark," Hawkman said in a low voice.

They were watching the area ahead, when someone yelled.

"Spike, get back here."

A couple of teenage boys appeared out of the woods carrying 22 pellet rifles over their shoulders. A young birddog bounded from the side and raced around the lads.

One of the boys grabbed the dog's collar. "Settle down. You're going to scare off any squirrels or rabbits."

Hawkman cupped his hand over his mouth. "Holster your guns and let's talk to those lads. Maybe they've seen the others. Let me do the talking." Stepping out from behind the tree, he raised a hand. "Hey, there."

Both boys jumped and pointed their guns at the men.

"Don't shoot. We're lost hikers," Hawkman said.

The boy, who looked the oldest, frowned. "I'm not sure I believe you. This here country is a long way from anywhere."

"We know, we've been wandering around for hours. You're the first humans we've come across. We got lost from our group and probably made a wrong turn. Have you by any chance seen two men and two women?"

Both boys shook their heads and shouldered their rifles. "Nope."

"How do we get out of these woods?"

They pointed in the direction the men were headed. "Just keep going and you'll soon come to a creek. Follow it downstream and you'll come to a dirt road."

"How far?" Hawkman asked.

The older kid bit his lip. "Not sure, but not more than ten miles."

"Thanks for your help. We better get to walking; we've got a ways to go."

The men continued forward, passing the two teens and their dog.

Chandler glanced over his shoulder at the kids. "Wonder where they live?"

"Probably in a cabin nearby," Hawkman said. "They didn't appear to be city kids; seemed to know the area."

"They hadn't seen the foursome," Owens said. "I hope we're on the right track."

Hawkman glanced at the officer. "My hunch is those boys had just left on their hunting excursion, and since they came out of the woods from the South, probably missed our motley crew."

"I sure hope they gave us the right directions," Chandler cut in. "I don't cherish trooping through the forest back to Harmon's in the dark."

Hawkman swatted at a buzzing insect, took off his hat and wiped the sweat from his forehead. "We'll soon know."

The men walked for another thirty minutes, then Hawkman halted and cocked his head. "Hear that?" he asked.

"What does it sound like?" the detective asked.

"Running water."

Owens grinned. "Music to my ears."

"Damn, I must be going deaf in my old age," Chandler said. "Can't hear it."

"Too many guns shooting near your head," Hawkman said. "Plays havoc with the hearing."

As they approached the stream, they grew quiet and stayed under cover until they could see the water. Checking the banks, they found shoe and dog prints where their robbers had crossed the narrow brook to the opposite side. The tracks led downstream.

Each man quickly splashed his face, which cleaned off the sweat and revived their spirits. They returned to the edge of the trees, stayed in the shadows, and followed the crooked river.

***

Glen led the way following the creek downhill. Annie and Babs stumbled along between the two men. Babs had put the leash on Lucy, fearing Glen with his hot temper might just shoot at her pet for the fun of it. She hated the long-haired man for slapping her and threatening her mother.

"Come on, ladies, you're dawdling, and we can't afford to waste time," Howy said, as he pressed on.

"We're getting very tired," Annie said. "How about a break?"

"Not yet. Just keep moving."

Babs touched her mother's arm and offered to take the backpack.

"It's too heavy, Hon. I'll manage."

"Looks like a road ahead," Glen yelled, and waved for them to hurry.

The three trotted forward, looking up and down the empty dirt path with weeds growing in the middle. To keep the stream from washing away the primitive road, the water ran through a large pipe and cascaded down the other side, dumping into a small canyon.

"There probably hasn't been a vehicle by here for days," Annie said.

"Well, we're going to be walking down it, just in case one comes by. It has to lead somewhere. It'll beat the hell out of stumbling through underbrush and fallen logs," Glen said.

"Aren't you afraid of being caught?" Annie asked.

Glen gave her a wicked smile, as his gaze roamed down her body. "Don't worry your pretty little head. Howy and I will take care of it."

Annie didn't like his answer, nor his action, and backed away.

"Okay, let's get moving," Howy said.

They moved onto the flat surface and kicked up dust as they walked between the tall trees on each side. Babs studied her mother's face; her mouth set in a hard frown and the wrinkle between her eyes had deepened. She appeared concerned. Babs had heard what Glen said, but she didn't understand the implications.

The sun continued across the sky and Babs watched a lizard as it dashed onto the road, then slipped back down the embankment as if to wait for the traffic to pass. Her gaze wandered toward the trees where birds flitted from limb to limb and a squirrel raced up the tree trunk.

She figured they'd sleep under the stars tonight, which she wouldn't have minded under different circumstances; but she didn't like the thought of being accompanied by these two criminals. Taking a deep breath, she kicked at the dirt under her feet, and wished she hadn't as a gust of wind sent it flying into her eyes. When she put her hand to her face, she felt a film of grit on her cheeks. Glancing down at her clothes, she gasped at how filthy her tennis shoes and jeans had become. Wading across the creek hadn't helped as dirt had clung to the damp cloth and dried in a caked mess.

Babs tried slapping at the crust of mud on her jeans; it didn't help, so she gave up. She looked down at her mother's feet and her clothes looked the same. Even Lucy's paws were coated with silt.

Abruptly, Lucy tugged on the leash. Her ears were on alert as she stared behind them. Babs glanced back and could see a vehicle coming in the distance. She patted her mother's arm and pointed.

"Glen," Howy yelled. "Pickup coming."

Everyone scooted to the side to let him pass. To Babs' surprise, Glen leaped into the middle of the road and waved his arms.

The truck came to a halt. An old man with gray hair and a long white beard leaned his head out the window. "What's the problem, young feller?"

"I need your pickup," Glen said, grabbing the door handle, and pointing his gun at the senior's nose.

The geezer tried to hang onto the door, but he was no match for Glen, and almost fell out as it swung open. Babs moved forward, but Annie grabbed her arm.

"Stay out of it. You could get hurt."

Feeling her owner's anxiety, Lucy growled and pulled on the leash. Babs reined her in and made her stay close.

Howy grabbed the keys from the ignition, then pulled the old fellow from the cab.

"If you're going to steal my truck, at least let me have my cane so I can get home."

Glen reached inside and tossed the stick down the road several feet away. "Don't want you to get any ideas about whopping me on the head."

Babs glared at Glen. When he pushed his gun into his pocket, she noticed the money belt around his waist. She turned and watched the old man limp toward his cane, pick it up and continue in the direction he'd come without ever looking back.

CHAPTER TWENTY-ONE

Hawkman, Chandler and Owens climbed onto the road. Chandler shaded his eyes and peered down the long span of dirt.

"Wonder how far ahead of us they are?" he asked.

"Hard to say," Hawkman said, strolling over to the other side of the stream. "These tracks look fresh. It's definitely them, as they're accompanied by paw prints. They're headed west."

Owens pointed. "There's a lone figure walking, or I should say, limping toward us."

Hawkman twisted his head around. "Maybe he's seen them."

The men hurried toward the person and soon were standing in front of the gray haired, long bearded man. The old fellow lifted his cane over his head.

"Don't come any closer. I'm not going to be robbed again."

"You say, you were robbed?" Chandler asked. "We're police; maybe we can help." He and Owens immediately displayed their badges.

"You ain't going to be much good on foot. They took my truck."

"Tell us what happened," Hawkman said. "First, let's get in the shade."

They meandered over to the edge of the forest where a large fallen log made an ideal resting place. The old man placed his cane beside his leg, took off his straw hat, wiped his face and bald head with a red bandana stuck in the bib pocket of his overalls, then plopped the hat back on. Hawkman handed him a bottle of water from the pack.

"Thank ya."

"Where do you live?" Chandler asked.

He pointed a crooked finger up the road. "About a mile from here, up the hill, in a wood cabin. Lived there for the past twenty years and never been bothered by robbers."

"Did they steal your truck from the cabin?" Owens asked.

The geezer shook his head. "No, I was headed to town to pick up some supplies when I saw this parade of people and a dog hiking along. A tall, lanky, long-haired man, jumped into the middle of the road and waved his hands for me to stop. When I did, he pointed a gun at me and yanked me out of the truck; said he needed it."

"Tell me about the others," Chandler said.

"Looked like a woman and her daughter. The dog must have belonged to the girl, as she had a leash on her. The other man was not very tall; his hair was real short and he had huge ears. If he could have waved them, he would have probably flied." The old man slapped his thigh and laughed. "Funniest lookin' guy I've ever seen. They were all very dirty."

"Did the women appear threatened?" Hawkman asked.

"I had the feeling they wanted to help me, but seemed afraid of the tall guy."

"What's your name?" Owens asked.

"Ed Bassett."

"Mr. Bassett, we're thankful you weren't hurt, and sorry we have no vehicle or we'd take you home."

"None of that 'Mr.' Just call me Ed. Walking home is no problem; it's getting my supplies that worries me. Also, were those men dangerous?"

"They robbed a bank in Yreka, kidnapped the women for hostages, and we're trying to catch them. Now it's going to be tougher since they have wheels." Hawkman said.

Ed ran his hand down his long beard. "Well, if they don't treat Mary Beth right, she'll conk out on them, and they'll be stranded."

Hawkman dropped the backpack to the ground and fished out a couple of sandwiches. "If I can find my way back out here, I'll take you to get your supplies; meanwhile, maybe this will hold you for the evening.

"Give us a description of your vehicle," Chandler said.

"It's a1973 faded green Chevy pickup. A few dents and rust spots, but runs like a charm, if treated gently."

Hawkman had been studying the road. "Ed, you say you live a mile or so away. Does this trail end at your place?"

"No, it goes for several miles and if my memory serves me right, it ends at Harmon Getty's place."

"Really? Well, that settles it, I'll be able to find you. Do you have a phone?"

"Nope, no electricity either. We don't have those luxuries out here in the boonies."

"Are you going to be home tomorrow?"

"I sure ain't goin' nowhere without my Mary Beth."

"We'll get your supplies tomorrow."

"Thank ya, much obliged." Well, gentlemen, I'm going to be on my way. Hope you find my pickup. I'm going to be lost without it."

With that, Ed Bassett tucked the sandwiches into the big pockets in his overalls, picked up his cane and headed home.

Hawkman snapped his fingers. "Chandler, do you know how to call the helicopter pilot?"

"Sure, what have you got in mind?"

"Certainly no reason for us to follow the hoodlums on foot any farther. The copter could land on the road. All he has to do is follow the throughway leading out of Harmon's place and he'll see us here in the open."

"Great idea. I sure didn't cherish the idea of heading back through the forest at night. Now, let's just hope we can get a signal," the detective said, as he unhooked the phone from his belt. "I know we were able to call out from Harmon's, so there must be a tower on one of these hilltops."

Chandler moved around until he got some bars indicating power. He punched in the number and put the phone to his ear. When he connected with Dan Wren, the pilot, he gave a thumbs up to Hawkman and Owens. After giving instructions on where they were, he hung up.

"It shouldn't take him long to get here, as he'll come as the crow flies." Hawkman said.

Owens glanced down the road. "You know we still have plenty of light. If he could swing down this path; maybe we'd spot the old man's truck."

Hawkman nodded. "They've been on their way for close to an hour. All depends on how fast the vehicle travels."

Chandler kept his eye on the sky. "It wouldn't hurt to give things a look. Ed said it would conk out if not treated gently. I doubt those two men know the meaning of the word. And who knows how much gas is in the tank. Their whole plan is to get out of these hills alive and to freedom."

Hawkman kicked a pebble down into the small canyon below. "My worries are about Annie and Babs. They're holding them as hostages. Since we can't shoot, they'll force the women to go with them, as they make their getaway."

"True, but we can at least keep tabs on them," the detective said.

About that time, the men heard the rotor noise of the helicopter overhead. They all gazed upward as the aircraft settled to the dirt road and landed not far from them.

The pilot talked in a loud voice as they climbed aboard. "You guys weren't hard to find. Harmon told me exactly how to get here."

Chandler leaned toward Dan. "Follow this road for a ways and we'll see if we can spot Ed Basset's truck. We'll tell you all about it when we get back to Harmon's."

Dan gave him a thumbs up and once the men were all loaded, he pulled up, then headed west. "I can't fly real low because of all the trees and hills."

"No problem," Chandler said. "We have our binoculars."

They traveled for several miles and spotted nothing, even at the small settlement which consisted of what looked like a feed store, market, gas station, and of all things, a MacDonalds set on the outskirts.

"Appears they didn't stop even for a little while. I don't see the pickup stalled anywhere, so it's still holding up; but they're long gone," Hawkman said.

"When we get back to the police station, I'll check the map and see where this road leads," the detective said. "Head home, Dan."

The pilot banked the helicopter back toward Yreka.

CHAPTER TWENTY-TWO

Dan set the aircraft down on the helicopter pad and turned off the rotors. "This has been quite an interesting adventure."

Chandler chuckled. "You can say that again."

"You want to join us for dinner?" Hawkman asked.

"No, thanks," Dan said. "The sandwiches you left for Harmon and me will last the rest of the evening. Speaking of Harmon, he is quite an interesting guy."

Owens patted Dan on the back. "Come on, and at least join us for a beer. I'd like to hear about the hermit."

The pilot laughed. "Ah, okay, you talked me into it."

The four men climbed out of the craft, and headed for their vehicles. Dan went with the detective and Officer Owens.

"You guys lead the way," Hawkman called.

They ended up at a place called 'Dave's Dive' well known for its seafood. The customers were a mix of young couples, middle aged families, and seniors. The interior walls were covered with what appeared to be red velvet with dim glowing lamps along the walls and a solitary lantern in the middle of each table. A soft blend of pleasant music filled the atmosphere and blocked out nearby conversation.

The four men picked a table in the corner and were immediately waited on by a male waiter dressed in black pants and a white shirt, complimented by a red vest. They each ordered a platter of fried shrimp, salad and a beer. While waiting for their food, they prodded Dan to tell them about Harmon.

Dan took a slug of beer. "When I met the hermit, I figured it would be a long boring day until you guys got back. It turned out to be anything but. Did any of you guys know why he ended up living out there in the boonies?"

Hawkman shook his head. "No, just figured he chose to."

"It's a bit more complicated. Many years ago, he didn't specify how many, he had a wife and a little girl. He worked as a manager of one of the major banks in Southern California, with high hopes of working up the ladder."

Chandler frowned. "Sounds like he had an education."

"Yeah, but you'd never know it looking at the long hair and beard, along with the no luxury place he lives. Would you believe, two Masters' degrees: one in business and one in math?"

Officer Owens placed his fork on his plate and wiped his mouth. "It sure goes to show; you can't tell by appearances."

A look of concern swept across Hawkman's face. "Something drastic happened to this man for his life to take such a turn."

Dan took a swallow of beer, and nodded. "It did. One day his wife and little girl stopped at the bank to see him. Just as they walked out of his office, gun shots erupted in the main lobby. Harmon dashed out, only to find his family in a pool of blood. Both dead."

"Oh, my God!" Hawkman said, wiping a hand across his face.

"As I'm sure you've assumed, a bank robbery had just taken place. But that's not the end of it. Harmon lost his will to live and vowed he'd find the three men who did this horrible deed. He had the robbers' pictures due to the surveillance cameras, and with the help of the police, found out their names. He researched their histories; the police were having no luck in finding them. When he thought he had enough information, and knew how to shoot any gun put in his hand, he sold his home, and started the fieldwork."

The three men had their focus fixed on Dan Wren.

"For crying out loud man, don't stop; continue," Chandler said.

"Had to wet my whistle, it was getting dry."

"You want another beer?" Hawkman asked, as their food arrived.

Dan waved his hand and shook his head. "No, I have to fly the helicopter back to the hanger. This is plenty."

"What happened next?" Owens asked.

"Harmon bought one of these little pop-up trailers, to pull behind his car, and started making his way across country to where he thought he'd find the murderers. It took him two years, but he found them. They were still together, pulling jobs; but they made a big mistake: they didn't pay any attention to the car trailing them, towing the small live-in box. When they came out of a bank, guns waving, they each met Harmon's bullets. After he killed them, he left, sold his car and trailer and eventually ended up where he is today."

"Damn, that's some story. You think he was telling the truth?" Owens asked.

Dan shrugged. "Why would he lie?"

"Wonder why he chose you to tell this to?" Chandler asked.

Hawkman, in deep thought, finished his last shrimp, and wiped his mouth with a napkin. "It appears to me, Harmon has carried this burden for years with no one to share his grief. We come along chasing bank robbers, who've taken a woman and her daughter as hostages, and it's brought these horrible memories to the surface. He needed to unload and would have probably used any one of us as his sounding board. It just happened to be Dan."

Dan pulled on his ear, and grimaced. "I agree. He also told me when his leg is better, if you guys haven't found the robbers, he's going after them."

Chandler drummed his fingers on the table. "Pray tell how he plans on doing that? He won't get far with a mule and wagon."

"I asked him the same thing," Dan said. "He told me, 'never you mind, I have my ways.'"

Some thoughts flashed through Hawkman's mind, but he remained silent until he could prove his point."

Dan pushed back his chair and stood. "It's been an eventful day, but I want to get the craft back to its home and tucked in so it's ready to use the next time we need it."

Hawkman shook his hand. "Thanks. You're a great pilot."

Dan nodded and smiled as he, Chandler and Owens rose to leave.

Chandler turned to Hawkman. "Once I can chart on a map where some of those
odd-ball roads lead, I'm throwing out another all points bulletin on the robbers. I'll include any county or town they might be passing through. I hope to get it done tonight."

"Tomorrow, I'll go pick up Mr. Bassett, and take him to pick up his supplies," Hawkman said.

"Tell him we hope to get his truck back in one piece."

***

Once on the road back to Copco Lake, Hawkman decided to go the long way and stop by Luke Jones'. He figured the man was sick with worry and had no way of knowing what had happened to his wife and child.

By the time he pulled in front of the Jones cabin, night had fallen. He could see a faint glow from the lantern coming through the windows. The nights were still chilly and he could smell the wood burning in the fireplace.

Luke's silhouette filled the front door. He held a rifle in his hands.

"Luke, it's Tom Casey."

The man rested the rifle against the wall and took his cane. "Come in. I hope you've got good news."

Hawkman stepped inside. "All I can tell you is Annie, Babs and Lucy are alive. Unfortunately, the robbers have stolen a pickup and escaped from us again. The search will resume when we get a bearing on where they're headed. The police are working on it."

Luke slumped down on the couch, and dropped his head into his hands. "I feel so helpless."

Hawkman reached over and patted his shoulder. "There's not a thing you could do."

"It's so quiet and lonely around here. I'm even happy to hear the rooster crow early in the morning."

Hawkman decided to change the subject. "Did your truck get delivered?"

"Yes, but the man wouldn't let me pay for it. He said it'd been taken care of."

CHAPTER TWENTY-THREE

Hawkman left Luke's and drove home. He felt sorry for the man, especially with him so crippled up, knowing he'd be nothing but a hinderance if he tried to join the search for his beloved family. At least he had his pickup and wouldn't feel so isolated.

When Hawkman reached home, Jennifer bombarded him with questions, particularly about Babs.

"I'm sure both she, Annie and Lucy are still safe. Their tracks are right alongside the two men as they clamor over the ground. Those guys won't harm the women as long as they're of value in assuring them a safe way to freedom. Getting the police off their tails is the biggest problem, but they may have made their odds better now, after stealing Mr. Bassett's truck."

"Who's Mr. Bassett?" Jennifer asked.

"An old codger who lives in those hills up around Harmon's." Hawkman related the story on how they discovered him. "I'm taking him to buy his supplies tomorrow. Detective Chandler has put out an all points bulletin on Bassett's truck and the two men who stole it."

"Do you have any idea where the robbers could be headed?"

"None. I'm not at all familiar with that area. The roads up there are mostly dirt. I want to get out my maps and see if I can figure out where they're headed. I doubt they know either, as Chandler said these guys weren't from this region; so I'm guessing they'll just follow any well-used path to get them into a more populated area. It looks as if Bassett's truck is holding up. So I figure if they find a paved street, they'll jump on it."

***

"Hurry and get in the pickup,"Glen ordered, as he pushed Annie. "You sit next to me." Then he pointed at Babs. "You scoot in next to your mom and take care of your dog.

Annie removed the backpack and shoved it toward the center, climbed in, then moved the bulky pack so it sat between her and Glen.

"Not room for me in the cab," Howy said, and climbed into the bed of the truck. "Don't take the curves too fast, I don't want to be thrown out."

Babs slammed the door shut, and had Lucy lie on the floorboard at her feet.

Ed Bassett had retrieved his cane, and stood watching several feet behind his truck. After they took off in a flurry of dust, Ed turned, shaking his head, and limped toward home.

Annie grabbed the dash. "Good grief, why are you going so fast over these country roads, they're rougher than a cob. You're jarring our insides."

"Shut up, woman. I want to get out of these damn woods."

"You jiggle this old truck too much, and the guts will start falling onto the road with a clatter; you won't get far, as it will conk out. I don't think you want to go back to walking."

Glen harrumphed.

Babs had to look out the window so he wouldn't see her grinning. Even though he didn't want them to think he'd listened, she noted he'd lifted his foot a bit from the accelerator.

"Where are we going?" Annie asked, pointing at the gas indicator. "If that gauge is right, it won't be far."

Glen glanced at the needle which quivered below a fourth of a tank. "Damn! Is there a place around here to get petrol?"

"I haven't the foggiest notion. I told you, I'm not familiar with this area."

"The old man was headed this way, and surely he wouldn't travel on a low tank if he couldn't buy gas to get home."

Annie nodded. "You're probably right."

When they crested a small knoll, Glen pointed ahead. "Hallelujah! Blacktop."

"Appears it goes west and east, so which direction are you going to take?" Annie asked.

"I'll decide when we reach it."

He soon rolled to a stop behind a painted stop sign. A small blue metal plaque straight in front of him had towns, mileage, and arrows listed in white, going both directions. "We're going west. Hamburg is only a couple or so miles. Surely it has a gas station."

Annie stared out the windshield, wondering if she'd ever see Luke or her home again. It didn't amount to much, but it belonged to her and Luke. She glanced at Babs and her heart swelled as she fought back the tears. The thought of her precious daughter being raped or murdered by these two criminals caused her stomach to roll. Maybe, once they were in contact with the public, some opportunity would present itself so she could get help. Right now, for Babs sake, she had to act strong and not afraid.

It didn't take long for them to reach the small burg. Glen pulled into the one and only gas station.

"Babs, Lucy and I need to go to the bathroom," Annie said.

Glen fired a look at her. "One at a time. Get your job done and get back out here pronto. I'll have Howy watch you."

Babs climbed out of the pickup and Annie handed her two cans of the meat products in the pack. "Feed Lucy and give her some water. Have her stay while you go to the restroom."

Instead of leaving her pet outside, Babs took her into the lavatory, pulled off a paper towel, and placed it on the floor. She popped off the tops of the cans and emptied them onto the towel. While Lucy ate, she took care of her business, then filled the basin with water; her pet was big enough to reach the sink by standing on her back legs. Babs also filled her thermos, cleaned up the mess, had Lucy go do her job behind the station, then hurried back to the truck, so her mom could tend to her needs.

Annie had listened to the service attendant as he approached Glen.

"See you've got Ed's truck."

"Yeah, we're visiting and he needed gas, so we offered to bring it down."

"Give him my regards."

Glen nodded. "Do you have a map of the area? We'd like to drive around before we head back."

"Sure," the attendant said, as he walked into the building

When they were all back in the truck, Glen pulled out of the station and into a parking spot in front of the big hardware store. He dashed in and ran back within minutes carrying two huge bags which he tossed into the bed of the truck with Howy.

"Make sure these don't blow out."

When they reached the edge of town, Glen pulled through the MacDonald's fast food drive-thru and ordered hamburgers, fries and drinks for all. Once on the road again, he took Highway 96 west.

Glen pointed to a sign at the side of the road. "How far are we from Happy Camp?"

"Thirty-two miles," Annie said.

"You know anything about this place?" he asked.

"I've heard about it, but never been there. It's located on the Klamath River."

"Do they have public campsites?"

"I think so."

They continued in silence as they ate.

Babs shared her fries with Lucy, and was glad they had something different to eat other than the canned meat. She'd been listening to the conversation between Glen and her mom, and figured they would stop at a campsite for the night. Without a blanket, the hard ground wouldn't be very comfortable. If the temperature dropped, she'd have to cuddle with Lucy and her mother. She wondered if they'd ever get back home to her dad, knowing he must be worried sick. Throwing off the sad feeling, she rolled up her trash in the sack the meal came in and tucked it between the seat and door.

CHAPTER TWENTY-FOUR

Trying not to crowd Babs too much, Annie adjusted the pack between Glen and herself. The stench of the man gave her a headache. All of them needed a bath, but his vile body odor had penetrated the cab. She wondered if he could smell himself. Even Babs had noticed and rolled down the window a tad.

Annie glanced out the back glass and could see Howy asleep, his head resting on the bags Glen had bought. "Why don't you and Howy take turns driving?"

He shot a look at her. "Are you telling me you don't like the way I smell?"

"Well, it would be good if we could all bathe," she said, meekly.

He let out a heinous laugh. "Not a chance, babe. I'm sure every law officer in the state is looking for us and this truck. The only way I'd be tempted to stop at a motel is, if you'd promise to take a shower with me."

Annie narrowed her eyes and glared at him. "Not a chance. You just keep driving until you fall asleep at the wheel, and then I'll take over."

"Where would you take us?"

"Straight to the nearest police station."

He jerked his head back. "Oh, my, you are one mean woman."

She turned her head toward Babs in disgust, and remained quiet.

***

Hawkman took a beer out of the refrigerator and moseyed over to his chair. Jennifer watched him with interest.

"What's on your mind?" she asked.

"How can you tell I've got something rattling around in my brain?"

She smiled. "For one thing, I've known you a long time; the second thing, you didn't ask if I'd like a gin and tonic."

He jumped up. "I'm so sorry, Hon. You're right, I'll fix you one pronto."

As he mixed her drink, she studied his face. "Want to tell me what's bothering you; maybe I can help."

"I'm not sure it's worth fretting over, but if we brainstorm a little, it might clear up a few questions."

They settled in the living room, and Miss Marple jumped off the hearth, wormed her way around Hawkman's boots, then gazed up at him with pleading eyes.

"Okay," he said. "If you'll be still, you can lay in my lap."

The feline immediately leaped onto his thighs and gave him a head butt on the chin.

"I thought you were going to teach her another way to show she loved me."

Jennifer laughed. "Don't think it's possible."

The cat settled down and Hawkman glanced at Jennifer. "Are you ready to hear what I'm stewing over?"

She swiveled her chair so she faced him. "Yes, go."

"I can't seem to get Harmon Getty, the hermit I've told you about, off my mind. It started the day he got shot by one of the men who kidnapped Annie and Babs. When we got there, he had lost a lot of blood and one of the officers found he could call for a medical helicopter."

She nodded. "You told me about the episode."

"What puzzled me, the flat spot beside his house looks like a copter pad. He knew the longitude and latitude of his area, and he had lanterns to use for the landing."

"Why is it puzzling?"

"I have this feeling the pad is there for a reason, but I didn't see any sign of an aircraft around his place. When I asked him how he got into town for supplies, he said he uses a wagon and his mule, which I saw."

"Has he ever mentioned friends coming to see him?" Jennifer asked.

Hawkman shook his head. "When we left the police helicopter there while chasing those kidnappers, the pilot stayed with Harmon. He said he had a very pleasant time with the hermit, as he told him about his personal life. Harmon lost his wife and little girl to bank robbers where he worked. He quit his job, sold his home, went looking for the murderers, found and killed them. Now he lives as a hermit with his three bloodhounds."

Jennifer frowned. "There are many loose ends to the story. Why don't you see if you can find him on the computer?"

"You're a genius, my beautiful wife. I'll do it right now, then hit the sack. I have a busy day tomorrow. I might even find out more information while taking Ed Bassett to buy his supplies." He got up from the chair and let out a yowl. Miss Marple's claws had gone through his jeans as she tried to hang on for dear life. "I forgot you were there," he said, quickly sitting down to lift her from his lap.

Once the debacle between Miss Marple and Hawkman ended, he hurried back to his home office, and booted up the computer. He removed his hat, hanging it on the peg beside his desk, flipped up his eye-patch and set to work. Using special passwords he'd acquired from being in the Agency which allowed him to access services no one else could. In the search box, he typed the name 'Harmon Getty'. He stared at the screen as it went through its hunt. Soon eight names popped up, but none had 'Harmon' or 'Getty' together. He printed them out and decided to check each one separately, hoping to find a picture, along with a description or narrative of the man's life. However, with all the hair Harmon had on his face and head, it would be difficult to compare him with a well-groomed individual.

Hawkman yawned as he worked his way through the list. When he hit the seventh name, Ronald Getty, he instantly became alert. The picture of the man, displayed at the side of the page, looked familiar. He couldn't put his finger on why, but when he read the history, he knew he'd found the real Harmon Getty. Printing out the information, he placed it beside the computer and prepared to go into a deeper search.

After two hours of combing through secure websites, Hawkman rubbed his eyes and leaned back in the chair. He thumbed through the printed data and realized he had enough to write a book on Harmon. Quite an impressive man. Putting it into a file, he shut down the computer and went to bed.

The next morning, after only four hours of sleep, Hawkman staggered into the kitchen and put on a big pot of coffee. He'd definitely be taking a thermos with him today. The sun's beams were peeking over the eastern hills and the wildlife began making their early noises. He yawned as he gazed out the window. Miss Marple wound around his ankles and let out a big meow.

Hawkman put a finger to his lips. "Ssh, let's not wake up your mistress. I'll get your food." He poured her bowl full and checked her water, which reminded him to check Pretty Girl's pans.

Barefooted, he made a quick trip out on the deck to the aviary; he pulled back the tarp that protected the falcon from the cold nights. The bird squawked as usual, wanting to go hunting. "Sorry, girl, not today. You're going to have to be satisfied with store bought stuff. I don't even have a tidbit in the freezer. I'll remedy it soon, I promise."

His feet freezing, he danced back into the house and poured himself a steaming cup of coffee. As the warm vapor circled his nose, he inhaled the rich aroma. He gobbled down a bowl of dry cereal, filled his thermos, dressed and got on the way to Ed Bassett's place.

Hawkman had no trouble in finding the log cabin. It sat on a small knoll on the other side of the bigger hill which Bassett had told him about. A thin column of smoke rose skyward from the chimney. When he climbed out of the vehicle, a delicious odor hit his nostrils. He knocked on the thick wooden door. A dog yipped two or three times.

"Hush up, Tippy. You'll scare our company away, the Lord knows we get very little," Ed said, as he pulled open the heavy plank. He squinted at the figure before him. "Why Mr. Casey, you're here earlier than I expected. Come in."

When Hawkman stepped into the cozy room, a tiny rat terrier Chihuahua bared her teeth and growled.

"What do we have here?" Hawkman asked.

"This is Tippy. She's harmless, but thinks she's my bodyguard; but I have my doubts," Ed said, laughing. "You had breakfast?"

"A bowl of dry cereal."

"That's not a meal, I'd call it a snack." He took a plate from the cupboard, filled it with scrambled eggs, slab bacon, and skillet toast, then set it down in front of Hawkman.

"I could smell the bacon frying when I climbed out of my 4X4. Just hoped you hadn't eaten it all."

Bassett smiled. "Enjoy, then we'll go to town."

CHAPTER TWENTY-FIVE

After the hearty breakfast, Hawkman pushed himself away from the table and patted his gut. "That should last me all day." He carried his plate to the bucket of water in the sink.

"Just drop it in and let it soak. I'll take care of the dirty dishes when I get home. It'll give me something to do," Ed said, as he placed a bowl of food on the floor for Tippy.

The two men soon left in Hawkman's vehicle and headed toward Highway 96. Ed instructed him how to get to the little town of Hamburg.

"It's just a hole in the road, but has everything a man needs to survive in these hills, so I seldom have to go any farther."

"What made you move to the boonies?" Hawkman asked.

The silence that ensued caused Hawkman to glance at the shaggy haired figure. He swore he could see tears in the corners of the man's eyes as he stared out the passenger side window.

"The question brings back sad memories," Bassett said.

"Don't feel like you have to answer. My curiosity may have stepped over the line."

Ed waved a hand. "No problem; it's probably good for me to talk about it. At times I get very lonely and feel sorry for myself. Harmon and I have had similar life experiences."

"I don't know a lot about Harmon."

"He and I lost our families in tragedies. His story is much more dramatic than mine, but it put us on the same level. We visit frequently, and he takes me for a ride in his helicopter."

Hawkman jerked his head around. "Harmon has a helicopter? I've never seen one on his property."

"He keeps it under his house. If you'll notice, his place sets up high and you have to go up several steps to get to the porch."

Hawkman nodded. "Yeah, now that you mention it, I can see where there would be a big space underneath. Sorry I interrupted, please continue your story."

"Where Harmon lost his wife and daughter by bank robbers, I lost a wife and son by a drunk driver who crossed the middle line and hit them head-on. They were killed instantly. I doubt they knew what happened."

Hawkman groaned. "Horrible! You have my condolences."

"Thank you. Life deals us pretty hard blows at times; but like Harmon, it knocked me off balance and I lost my desire to carry on. I would drive around endlessly, trying to put a purpose to my being alive. Then one day I came upon the log cabin. It had a 'for sale' sign in front. I walk around the property and peeked in the windows. I liked what I saw, so contacted the realtor. I moved in within a couple of weeks and have been much happier."

"I'm glad to hear things have worked out," Hawkman said, as he slowed down. "Looks like we're approaching Hamburg."

"Let's go down to the end of town first. There's a gas station run by a friend of mine. I'd like to find out if my pickup came through. It needed gas, and Frank would recognize my truck."

"Good idea," Hawkman said, pushing the accelerator. "I'll fill up while we're here."

He pulled up to one of the pumps and stopped. Ed grabbed his cane and climbed out of the 4X4, using the staff for balance.

Frank, the station owner, walked around the SUV, a big smile on his rugged face, and put out his hand. "Hey Ed, did you get your truck back in one piece?"

Bassett scowled. "So they did stop here?"

"They said they were your visitors and had offered to fill the tank if you would let them borrow it to look over the area. They bought a map too."

"They hi-jacked me up near my home, stole my truck and took off." He pointed to Hawkman. "This here is Tom Casey. He offered to bring me shopping until we can find my vehicle."

When Hawkman finished topping off the tank, the two men shook hands. "How many were in Ed's truck?" Hawkman asked.

"A tall guy in the cab with a woman, a young girl and a dog. A big guy sat in the bed."

"Did the women look okay?"

"They didn't appear hurt or anything, but I thought it weird when the guy told them they could only go to the bathroom one at a time."

As an after thought before leaving home, Hawkman had made copies of the sketches Babs had done of the men, and stuck them in his jeans back pocket." He took them out and showed them to Frank. "Do these resemble the males?"

He nodded. "Yep, that's them. Who are they?"

"They robbed a bank, and are using the women and the dog as hostages."

Frank wiped his face with a stained oil rag he had hanging out his back pocket, and faced Ed. "Sure wish I'd known, I'd have called the police."

"Did you happen to notice which way they went?" Ed asked.

Frank pointed toward the highway. "After going through the hamburger drive-thru, they went west on ninety-six."

Hawkman and Ed left the station and drove to the mercantile. Ed went through the store picking out supplies, while Hawkman showed the sketches to different sales persons. One recognized Glen and told how he'd hurriedly bought four sleeping bags and miscellaneous items, then paid in cash.

After Ed finished shopping at the hardware store, they went to the grocery market. Ed bought several items that needed refrigeration; Hawkman glanced at him with a questionable expression. "How are you going to keep those things cold?"

Ed smiled. "In my propane refrigerator."

"Have you told Harmon about this?"

"He already has one; that's where I got the idea."

"I must be losing my sense of observation," Hawkman said. "I didn't notice one in either of your places."

"It's because we have them in closets out of sight. Our places don't have much floor space. We need all the room we can get. The propane tank is at the back. You wouldn't have seen it when you came up the driveway."

"That's a relief; at least I feel better now," Hawkman said, laughing.

They drove back to the log cabin and Hawkman helped Ed carry all his supplies into the house. Ed's little dog, Tippy, sat on the couch, as if she knew to stay out of the men's way or she'd get stepped on.

"Mr. Casey, I certainly appreciate you doing this for me. These staples should carry me through for quite a spell. If I don't get my truck back soon, I'll have to start looking for a replacement."

"Would you like me to help you put things away?"

"No. You've done enough, and I have the rest of the day. Besides, I wouldn't know where everything is, if I didn't do it myself."

"I'll get out of your hair so you can get on with your chore. I'll check in on you periodically," Hawkman said, as he left.

The driveway had enough room for him to turn around his SUV so he could drive down front first on the sloping gravel road. When he reached the end, he headed toward Harmon's place. In his mind, he tried to analyze the difference between Ed Bassett and Harmon Getty. Obviously, Ed had money, and at first he thought Harmon had none. However, if he had a helicopter, he definitely had some.

It appeared Harmon tended to be more quiet mouthed about his personal life, whereas Ed talked a blue stream, not only about himself, but others too. After doing the research on Harmon, Hawkman realized the reason why he didn't want people too close. Maybe, if he went about it carefully, he could get Harmon to talk.

This could all come later. His first priority was to rescue Annie, Babs and Lucy. He needed to call Detective Chandler and give him the latest on the whereabouts of the foursome plus one. He pulled to the side of the road, in case he had to point the instrument toward a tower. It surprised him when the cell phone had strong bars. After contacting Chandler, he informed him of the trail to the bank robbers.

"You think they're on the way to Happy Camp?" Chandler asked.

"It appears that way, and probably sleeping in a campsite as Glen purchased four sleeping bags in Hamburg."

"The bad thing is, they're out of my territory," Chandler said. "I'll call the sheriff in Happy Camp and let him know the story. I'll also let him know you're on their tail."

CHAPTER TWENTY-SIX

Knowing he'd entered the Happy Camp area, Glen stayed alert, looking to find a place to spend the night before dark. He wanted a campsite among the trees so the truck wouldn't be exposed to traffic. Soon he spotted a small sign with an arrow stating 'campground'. He turned and drove about a half block into the woods. There were several vacant sites with concrete picnic tables and fire pits. The evenings and nights were still pretty cold; not quite warm enough for family outings, which suited him. He didn't need a bunch of snotty-nosed kids running around asking stupid questions.

Selecting a site, he backed the truck next to the table so the front end faced the road, in case he needed a fast getaway.

"Okay, everyone, get out and stretch your legs before it gets too dark. We'll be spending the night here."

Babs and Lucy hopped out. Babs stretched, then found a stick to throw for Lucy to retrieve. She didn't pitch it far nor wander away from the truck. Annie climbed out, leaving the backpack of canned meats on the seat, ran in place to loosen up her leg muscles, then swung her arms around to ease the tension in her neck and shoulders. She moved toward Babs.

"If I see the opportunity for us to escape, I'll signal you," she whispered, keeping her back to the two men meandering around the truck.

Babs nodded as she watched her dog chase the small branch.

Lucy brought the stick to Annie, who took it, and pitched it a short distance. "Go get it, girl."

Babs touched her mother's arm, then made some signs of hearing water.

"It's the Klamath River across the road from where we came in. Right now, we're on the outskirts of Happy Camp." Annie pointed toward the empty campsite near them. "Look, there's a water spigot; wonder if it works."

They ran to it and found it a workable faucet. Babs turned it on and washed her face, then made a bowl with her hands so Lucy could drink. When they were both through, Annie washed her face and arms.

"Sure wish we had a washcloth, I'm sure I stink to high heaven. I almost gag sitting next to Glen in the truck," she laughed. "He's rancid."

Babs grinned, then suddenly, jerked up her head. Howy stood over them with his fists on his hips.

"Wondered where you ladies went. I'll walk you over to the public bathrooms."

It puzzled Babs why Lucy didn't react to Howy like she did to Glen. Probably because he'd never threatened her or her mom. Animals seem to have an uncanny sense, she thought, as they followed Howy behind their campsite. A rustic mirror of aluminum hung on the wall. Annie and Babs removed the bands from their pony tails, shook out their long hair, ran fingers through the tangled messes, then restored their pony tails. They were soon back at the truck and Annie suggested Babs feed Lucy.

She climbed into the cab and fumbled through the canned meats in the pack; pulling out a couple of small cans for herself and her mom, she smiled when she pulled out a can of dogfood. The people who owned the hunter shacks must have had pets. Fortunately, all the cans had flip-tops and were easy to open. Babs dumped Lucy's food on the cement that held the table. While her dog devoured the treat, Babs and her mom nibbled on the Vienna sausages.

The shadows were getting long, and shafts of sunlight poked through the middle of the trees. Little by little the streaks turned off.

Glen walked over to Annie. Lucy bared her teeth, and growled low in her throat. Babs placed a hand on her pet's back, which seemed to play a calming role.

"It's time to hit the sack, as we'll be on the road before sun-up tomorrow. So Annie, you'll sleep with me and Babs will nestle with Howy."

Annie threw back her shoulders, and glared at him. "Like hell we will. My daughter and I will sleep together with our dog. You and Howy can go jump in the river to cool off."

Glen narrowed his eyes and grabbed Annie by the hair. "You'll do what I say."

As he started pulling Annie toward the truck, she kicked and fought like a panther; digging her long fingernails into his arms and tried to reach his eyes, all along screaming.

Babs jumped up, remembered the pocket knives she'd put in her pocket before leaving home, brought one out, and opened it; while Lucy barking and nipped at Glen's ankle with her teeth.

"Call the damn dog off or I'll kill your mother," he yelled, kicking out at Lucy.

He dropped the tailgate of the pick-up and pushed Annie against it. He held her down with his legs as he yanked the bottom of her sweatshirt over her head, pinning her arms, then grabbed her breast.

Babs suddenly let out a scream, "No! no! no!" She held the knife in an attack mode, and ran toward him, jabbing his shoulder. He staggered backwards, then fell on his butt moaning and holding his arm. Sobbing, Babs grabbed her mother, and pulled down her sweatshirt. Annie, tears rolling down her checks, wrapped her arms around her daughter and hugged her tightly.

Howy was sauntering down the trail from the bathroom, until he heard the commotion coming from their campsite. He picked up his speed and ran toward the truck. As he rounded the table, he saw Glen rolling on the ground in a blood soaked tee shirt.

"Shit!" he said, as he knelt beside him. "What the hell happened?"

"She stabbed me," he gasped. "I can't reach the knife. Can you pull it out?"

"Shouldn't we get you to the hospital?"

"Dammit, Howy, I'm not going to any medical center. The police will be called in and we end up spending the rest of our lives in jail. Just get the blasted knife out."

Howy eased the blade out of Glen's back and the blood ran. "You're really bleeding bad."

"Shit, put pressure on it; I can't do it myself."

Howy pulled the tail of Glen's shirt up, wadded it and put the cleanest area he could find over the wound and pressed."

Glen sucked in his breath. "I think I saw a small first aid kit in the glove compartment. Have Annie get it."

Howy glanced up at the women, who appeared hypnotized at the sight before them.

"You heard him. Check the glove compartment."

Babs pulled herself from the locked grip her mother had around her, gave Lucy the command to stay, ran to the front of the truck and climbed into the cab. She found the kit and took it to Howy.

"You're going to have to open it," he scowled. "You can see my hands are covered in blood."

Babs popped it open. "I don't know what size bandage you need."

Howy glanced at her. "When did you start talking?"

"Just a few minutes ago. When Glen tried to rape my mother."

"Did you stab him?"

Babs narrowed her eyes. "Yes, and I'd do it again if he tries so much as to touch her. But next time, I'd make sure it kills him."

"Where'd you get the knife?" Howy asked.

"I had it in my pocket."

Annie had moved up next to Babs and took the kit into her hands. She took a large piece of gauze, folded it, and put some ointment on it. "Move your fingers and I'll bandage the wound."

She had Howy hold the corners of the gauze while she pulled off pieces of tape and cut it with her teeth. She soon had the laceration covered.

"He's so filthy, it wouldn't surprise me if it didn't get infected. He really needs to see a doctor for stitches and an antibiotic."

Glen rolled over and sat on his butt. His face had turned pale, but around his eyes and mouth, the flesh had taken on a green color. "I'll take my chances."

He pushed himself up with his good arm, but almost fell over. Howy grabbed him before he hit the ground.

"You've lost a lot of blood. Better take it easy," Howy said.

While Howy tended to Glen, Babs picked up her knife off the ground where Howy had tossed it, wiped it off on the grass, then cleaned the blade by running it across her jeans. She closed the blade and stowed it back into her pocket.

CHAPTER TWENTY-SEVEN

Babs watched Howy help Glen, who continuously moaned and groaned, climb into the cab of the truck. She secretly wished he'd fall out and land on the knifed shoulder, but it didn't happen.

Night had fallen and as Howy backed away from the pickup, he suddenly stopped and watched a shaft of light working its way through the darkness about a half block away.

He quickly turned to Annie and Babs. "Get in the truck, we're getting out of here." He directed Annie into the cab and put Babs and Lucy in the bed. He slammed the tailgate.

"Get under those bags and stay hidden, regardless of what happens." He hopped into the driver's side and drove out of the campsite.

"What the hell's going on?" Glen asked.

"I'm sure the police are looking for us. There's a vehicle over a row or so, shining a flood light into each site checking who's occupying it. We need to get behind them or into a different area."

"Try not to hit so many bumps," Glen complained.

"Shut up your whining."

"Where's the kid and her dog?"

"In the back."

"Aren't you afraid she's apt to jump out?"

"Not with her mother up here with you. She'd like to do you in."

Howy pulled out on the main highway and headed southwest.

Annie had shifted the backpack full of the canned food so it rested between her and Glen. She didn't fear Howy like she did Glen, and didn't care if the bag shifted and hit him on the wounded shoulder. In fact she might even help it a bit if the advantage warranted itself. She felt pride in her brave daughter; and hopeful since her voice had returned. Glancing through the rear window, she could see Babs' arms wrapped around Lucy as they huddled under those bags.

Glen winced at every turn. "This is the roughest damn truck I ever rode in."

"Don't be such a wimp," Howy said.

"Easy for you to say; you didn't get stabbed. I hope you took the knife away from the brat."

"Yep, threw it in the bushes."

***

Hawkman stopped in front of Harmon's. The place appeared quiet; even the bloodhounds didn't warn of his arrival with their haunting bays. As he jogged up the steps, he peeked under the porch only to discover the dogs were not there. He knocked on the door; received no response even after calling out Harmon's name. Trying the knob, he found it locked, then peered into the window to be sure Harmon wasn't lying on the floor; hurt or dead.

Not seeing any sign of life, he jogged down the steps and walked toward the back of the house. The mule occupied his pen, standing under the shed out of the direct sunlight. The water tub was filled to the brim and set in a corner of the lean-to. The wagon Harmon had told Hawkman he used for his supplies, rested near the gate.

Hawkman continued his journey around the house. He studied the width and depth of the construction and agreed with Ed; there would be room to store a small helicopter under the floor. Examining the wall, he noticed runners on the top and bottom of what looked like a long sliding door. He followed it to the end and found it flush with the jamb. Trying to work his fingers between the boards, he could tell, after further inspection, two locks held it firm; one at the bottom and one at the top. They appeared to be the type that locked when closed and would need a key to open. He could also hear what sounded like a generator.

As he backed away from the big sliding door, his gaze dropped to the ground. He could make out tracks in the scrubby grass leading to the flat spot; probably made by attached wheels and a hand-held tow bar to move the aircraft to what Hawkman now dubbed a helicopter pad.

He strolled around the side of the cabin and toward the front, wondering if Harmon had taken the dogs with him or whether they were out hunting. Climbing the steps, he decided to wait a while. He doubted Harmon would land in the dark without the lanterns, as it could prove to be quite risky.

Hawkman settled into one of the ragged overstuffed chairs on the big porch, and looked out over the breathtaking landscape of the hills surrounding Harmon's house. The sunbeams danced in and out of the trees glancing off the swaying leaves. A child's imagination could run wild with the rays trying to catch the squirrel or bird hopping from limb to limb. The breeze had a nip, but not enough to make you cold, just enough to soothe the nerves after a long day.

He scooted to the edge of the cushion and listened intently. He swore he could hear the baying of dogs in the distance. Following the sound with his gaze, he studied the edge of the wooded area, and sure enough, running toward the house were Harmon's three bloodhounds. The one in the front, with his ears flopping in the wind, held his furry prey between his jaws. His two companions were howling as they followed. They scuttled under the porch without giving Hawkman a second look. He could hear the angry scuffle that ensued, and wondered which dog had won, but didn't dare peek.

The snarling finally subsided, and Hawkman concentrated on the sounds of the sky. The sun slowly sank toward the top of the hills, and he wondered if he'd made a mistake expecting Harmon to drop out of the sky in a helicopter. He definitely couldn't see what the man had stored below the house, only Ed Bassett's word and tracks that indicated a heavy item had been rolled out.

Hawkman got up and paced the porch. Maybe a friend had picked up Harmon, and taken him to town. Any number of things could be the reason why he wasn't home. He checked his watch and realized he'd already been there an hour. He'd wait a few more minutes then head home. As he stood, he slipped his hands into the back pockets of his jeans, and rested one foot on the railing around the porch; his cell phone vibrated. It surprised him, as he'd forgotten the police had been able to get a signal from Harmon's house.

Detective Chandler's voice greeted him, and relayed he'd spoken with the sheriff of Happy Camp and his team had searched all the campsites with no success. This didn't surprise Hawkman, as it seemed these two robbers had a talent of staying one step ahead of the authorities. He hoped Annie and Babs were still safe.

After hanging up, he thought about where these men might be taking the two females, and what they had in mind for them. Did they have a plan or were they just keeping ahead of the cops? Would they continue south on Highway 96 or head off on a side road? If they could just spot Ed's pickup, and a helicopter would be the ideal machine to do the job. However, the police department being strapped for funds, would never give permission to use the aircraft for following these two.

Hawkman exhaled and slid his phone into the pouch on his belt. He'd just about decided to leave Harmon's when his ear caught the faint slap of helicopter rotors. He quickly moved to the edge of the porch and searched the sky. The dogs began to bay as though they recognized the sound. Hawkman smiled to himself as he saw a small copter passing over a low hill and angling toward the house. He knew Harmon would recognize his SUV in front of the house, and wondered what his reaction would be.

Watching the craft set down in a perfect landing on the pad, Hawkman waited until the rotors quit spinning before he jogged down the porch stairs. It surprised him when Harmon glanced at him.

"Any news on Annie and Babs?"

"No. It appears the Happy Camp patrol had no luck in searching the camp grounds."

"I didn't have any luck on my search either," Harmon said, as he fiddled with the helicopter.

Hawkman raised his brows. "You were hunting for them too?"

"Yeah, but I didn't have any idea they'd gotten as far as Happy Camp. How'd you find out?"

Hawkman gave him a rundown on the clues. "We figured they'd be camping out due to the purchase of the four sleeping bags; it's at least a sign the women are safe. They either pulled a good one on the police, or traveled past the camp grounds."

Harmon listened closely, then stepped away from the helicopter. "I was going to ask you to help me put Baby Jane away, but think I'll leave her out tonight."

"Baby Jane?" Hawkman asked.

Harmon grinned and pointed to the machine. "My baby copter."

Hawkman chuckled. "I'll sure be happy to help."

"I have a better idea," Harmon said. "Why don't you come about six in the morning with your knowledge of where those hoodlums have taken Annie and Babs. We'll take off in Baby Jane, and see if we can't track them down."

"I'll be here," Hawkman said.

CHAPTER TWENTY-EIGHT

Howy soon drove past the boundaries of Happy Camp. His eyelids kept drooping and he knew he needed some sleep or he'd end up running off the road or into an oncoming car. He soon spotted some mailboxes lined up along the road and turned onto the dirt lane beside them. Following it for about a mile, he pulled over and stopped in front of a gate which looked like it protected a path leading into a field.

Glen had his head resting against the passenger window with his eyes closed. When the truck came to a stop, he jerked and groaned. "Why are we stopping?"

"I've got to get some rest or I'm going to fall asleep at the wheel."

"Where are we?"

"On a country road, a mile or two off of Highway 96."

Glen peered out the window. "You think we're safe?"

"Hell of a lot more than back at the campsite with the park patrol nosing around."

***

Annie remained quiet, but wondered what kind of sleeping arrangements these two would make. No way did she want to be stuck in the cab with Glen, even though his injury would prevent him from doing any horsing around. Not only did he stink, but she didn't like the man, and wanted no part of him.

***

"Get out those sleeping bags I bought, and distribute them. It's going to get cold tonight," Glen said, as he tried to move.

Howy climbed out of the truck, and bent over the rail of the bed. He grabbed one of the sacks and pulled out two rolled up bags.

Meanwhile, Annie scooted out right behind Howy and in doing so, the backpack, partially full of the canned meats fell over and hit Glen's shoulder. He let out a scream of agony.

Howy poked his head back into the cab. "Good Lord, Glen, you're going to wake up the dead."

"Put this damned thing in the back."

While Howy struggled to open one of the bed rolls for Glen, Annie pulled the pack across the seat, took out a few cans of meat, then swung it into the bed. She then went to the back of the truck and dropped the gate.

"Hey, what are you doing?" Howy called.

"I'm going to let Lucy go do her business," Annie said, as the dog jumped out. Then we're going to have a bite to eat."

He nodded, then turned his attention back to the sleeping bag.

Babs slipped out behind her pet, glanced at Howy, then whispered to her mom. "Maybe tonight we'll have a chance to escape."

Annie smiled. "You must be reading my mind," she said in a low voice.

Howy finally backed away from the pickup, shaking his head. "Glen's teeth are chattering and he's saying crazy things."

"He's probaby delirious with a high fever, and needs to see a doctor," Annie said.

Howy shrugged. "It's out of the question."

"What if he dies? You just going to bury him out here in no man's land?"

He scowled as he stared at her. "Don't even talk like that."

Annie decided to change the subject. "Are we spending the night here?"

"Yeah," he said, reaching into the bed of the truck and pulling the other huge bag toward him. He brought out two more sleeping bags. "These are for you and your daughter."

"Thanks, at least we'll stay warm," Annie said, handing one to Babs. She cocked her head and looked at Howy. "What are the sleeping arrangements? Do not think for one minute of putting me or my daughter in the cab with Glen."

"Since the pickup has a bench seat, I think I'll let him have the whole thing. He needs some good rest where he can spread out. The three of us, and I assume your dog, will sleep in the bed of the truck." He put his hands up. "Don't worry, I'll sleep against the rear gate and you gals can have the head area."

Annie studied the sky. "I think we better get our beds fixed while we can still see. It's going to be darker than mud in about thirty minutes and we won't be able to find our hand in front of our face." Then she frowned. "I sure don't like the looks of those clouds; we could have a storm roll in."

She and Babs smoothed out their beds, then Annie took the large plastic bag, tore a slit at the top with her teeth, and ripped it down the side. As she reached the bottom, she could tell there was something else in the bag. She fumbled around with her hand and could feel the outline of a flashlight, and a box, which she assumed held batteries. Slipping them out, while Howy looked the other way, she tucked the items into the sleeping bag. She then spread the plastic over the top of their beds to protect them, in case it should rain. Howy followed suit as he watched what the women did.

When they finished, they hopped over the railing and leaned against the fender as they opened a couple of cans of Vienna Sausages. Babs shared her water with her mom. Howy rummaged through his backpack, grabbed a can of ground meat, which he ate by spooning it out with the lid.

About that time, Lucy came bounding toward them, stopped directly in front, and gave herself a good shake, sprinkling the three with water.

"Oh, my gosh," Babs said, as she reached down to stroke her pet. "She's soaking wet."

"She's found a stream or pond. Too bad it's so danged cold," Annie said. "I'd go for a swim and clean off some of this dirt."

Babs opened a can of meat for Lucy. Once all had finished their meal, they tossed the empties into the gutter alongside the road.

Howy checked on Glen. "He's finally sleeping."

"Best thing for him," Annie said.

Suddenly, the heavens lit up and the rumble of thunder rolled across the sky.

"I think we better get under the plastic so we don't get drenched," Annie said. "It would be miserable to sleep in wet clothes."

Babs and her mother climbed into the back of the truck and under the plastic. Lucy jumped in behind them and hunkered down beside her mistress. "Oh, good, you're almost dry," Babs said, hugging her pet. As she wiggled down into the bag, her foot hit an object. Reaching down, she felt it and realized what it was. "Mom," she whispered. "There's a flashlight in my bedroll."

Annie quickly put a finger to her lips, and signaled Babs to leave it there.

About that time, Howy dropped the tailgate. Annie and Babs both jumped.

"What are you doing?" Annie asked.

"Being on this incline, if it rains, the water will drain out of the back and maybe we won't get soaked."

"Next time, warn us; it made the whole truck rock."

He chuckled. "You ladies sure are skittish." He walked toward the front of the truck. "I'll be right back; don't do anything foolish. I'll be able to see you if you get out of the pickup."

After he strolled away from the truck, going down the dirt road, Babs quickly pulled out the package of batteries. "You keep an eye on him and I'll install these while he's gone." She fished out one of her pocket knives and slashed the container open. Once she put the batteries in, she aimed the light down into her sleeping bag and flipped it on.

"This is great," she said, turning it off; then dropped the light and packaging into her bedroll.

A loud whack on the glass of the back window of the cab caused Annie and Babs to jerk around. They both screamed; Lucy growled, barked and bared her teeth. Glen had his tongue pressed against the glass, making his face look distorted. His eyes were glassy and darting from side to side; the hair on his head stood out like he'd been electrocuted. It didn't help when a bolt of lightning struck a tree not far away, making a horrible crackling noise just as a loud roll of thunder passed over their heads.

Howy dashed to the truck just as a deluge of rain began to fall. "What the hell's wrong?"

Annie pointed at the glass.

"Oh, my God," he said, grabbing the handle to the driver's side door. He yanked it open and tried to subdue Glen as he kicked and thrashed about. "Glen," he yelled, "get control of yourself."

When nothing worked, Annie and Babs watched in horror as Howy hauled off and cracked Glen in the jaw, knocking him out cold. Glen went limp and Howy got him situated in the seat, then covered him with the sleeping bag.

He backed out of the cab into the rain, closed the door, and locked it. "I hated to do that, but he's a crazy man. He must have a really high temperature; his body felt terribly hot, like he'd just stepped out of the oven."

CHAPTER TWENTY-NINE

Annie watched Howy climb under the watershed in his area of the truck bed. It appeared his limbs were too heavy to operate. Not only was the man exhausted, but also disgusted. Annie prayed he'd fall into a deep sleep, and the rain would stop, giving her, Babs and Lucy a chance to escape. Tonight might be their only opportunity, rain or not. Glen still didn't emerge as a threat. If Howy didn't get him to a doctor or hospital soon, he might die.

She moved toward Babs. "Are you having trouble staying awake?" she whispered.

"No. Are we ready to go?"

"Not yet. We'll wait until we're sure Howy is asleep, and hopefully, this storm will pass. Don't forget the flashlight."

"I've got it in my hand."

Annie waited about fifteen minutes before she poked her head out from underneath the plastic sheeting. The rain had almost ceased and she could hear Howy's heavy breathing. "We'll give him a few more minutes to make sure he's in a deep sleep. When we scoot out of here, bunch up your bed roll so it looks like you're still in it," she said, still whispering.

Within a few minutes, Howy started snoring in a loud steady rhythm.

Annie took ahold of Babs arm, and said in a low voice, "It's time. Be as quiet as you can and try not to rock the truck anymore than necessary."

They each slipped out of their sleeping bags, fluffing them so they appeared full, then pulled the plastic sheet over where their heads would've been. Annie grabbed the backpack, which had a few more cans of meat, enough to keep them from being hungry for a few days. Babs followed her mother as they slid over the truck sides. Lucy bounded out quietly. Annie stopped a moment and listened; Howy's snoring continued without a break. She slipped the straps of the pack over her shoulders, took Babs hand and hurried up the road the way they'd come; Lucy trotted alongside.

After a few minutes, Annie looked back to make sure they were out of earshot of the truck. "We should get off this road in case Howy discovers we're gone and comes looking."

Babs flipped on the flashlight and studied the fence line, then turned it off, and clambered up a small mound to get to a weak section. She stepped on the bottom row and held up the barbed wire, then lit up the way for her mom and Lucy. Once they crawled through, Annie held it open for Babs.

"At least, we're not as vulnerable in the field," Annie said. "If we see any headlights, we can drop down in this tall grass and won't be seen."

"Where are we headed?" Babs asked.

"To the highway, where Howy turned off. It's not too far, because he told Glen he'd pulled in a mile or two, so the truck wouldn't be spotted. So we'll just follow the road."

"I hope Howy sleeps a long time."

"I think he will; he gave me the impression of complete fatigue. Glen is really sick, and I doubt he even knows where he is or what's happening."

They trudged along. The storm had moved away; the dark clouds had parted letting the moon beams shine through giving them enough illumination so they didn't have to use the flashlight.

Babs grabbed her mother's arm. "I see headlights coming up the road."

Both of them dropped to the ground on their stomachs. Since Lucy didn't recognize Babs' verbal commands yet, she signaled with her hand, and the dog went down on her belly. The two females peeked through the tall weeds as the vehicle passed.

"Do you think the person will stop at the parked truck up ahead?" Babs asked.

"I really doubt it," Annie said. "The truck looks empty, with Glen knocked out on the seat, and Howy asleep behind the tail gate; plus it's parked in a drive to a padlocked gate. They'll figure it's just someone checking their pasture."

"I sure hope so, I'd hate to think the field belonged to the guy who just drove by."

Annie grinned. "Me, too. Keep your fingers crossed."

They stood and brushed off the weeds stuck to the front of their clothes, took a swig of Babs' water, then continued their trek.

"Are we going to try to hitch a ride when we get to the highway?" Babs asked.

"No, it's too risky. I figure Howy will go south; we certainly want to avoid him and Glen. Thought we'd backtrack to Happy

Camp; it won't be too far. We've hiked longer distances. Once we're there, we'll find a store or a home and call the police."

"Sounds like a good plan to me."

When Annie and Babs reached the highway, they decided to cross over and walk facing the traffic. Not wanting car headlights to expose them, they stayed quite a distance from the edge of the road. There were few vehicles traveling this night, which satisfied Annie; the fewer the better.

The night had turned chilly, the sky remained clear of clouds and the moon glowed. Fortunately, both women were dressed warmly due to the heavy sweatshirts they'd acquired at the hunter's shack. Annie vowed to herself if they ever got home, she'd talk to the owners about the clothes and food they'd literally stolen and would promise to replace the items. Speaking of food reminded her they should stop and munch on something. The pack didn't seem nearly as heavy as it had originally; she hoped there was enough to feed the three of them at least one more time.

"Babs, let's take a break and have a bite to eat. We could use some extra energy."

They flopped down behind a grassy knoll so they wouldn't be seen by the traffic. Babs shined the flashlight into the bag and read the labels.

"Great, there's a can of dog food left." She dumped out the can of beef squares onto a flat rock for Lucy.

"What's left?" Annie asked.

"A can of Spam, which we could split, along with two cans of Vienna sausages and two of cooked beef and pork."

"Let's share the Spam," Annie said.

After they ate, Babs lay down and rested her head on Lucy's belly. "Man, I didn't realize how tired I am."

Annie lay down beside her. "Let's take a nap. I think we're safe here; and it won't do any good to get into Happy Camp if the stores aren't open, or if everyone is still asleep in their beds."

It didn't take long before all three were snoozing.

***

The sun's beams hit Howy's face and roused him out of a deep sleep. He pushed the bed roll off the rest of his body, and glanced up at the other two bags. It appeared the two women were covered from head to toe and still asleep. He climbed out of the truck bed and strolled up to the driver's side and peeked in the window. Glen's cheeks were fiery red. His chest rose and fell in short sporadic breaths; he still seemed to be very ill.

Howy looked back at the two sleeping and wondered why they hadn't moved; and he couldn't see evidence of the women's long hair. He reached over, pushed on the cloth and it sank to his touch. He yanked off the plastic coverlet, and discovered both bags were empty.

"Damn!" He hit the side of the truck with his fist. "I should have known they'd take advantage of me being so tired and Glen sick."

He scrounged around the truck bed and found his backpack with cans of edible food.

Taking out several cans, he unlocked the driver's side and slid into the seat.

Howy shook Glen's leg. "Wake up. You want something to eat?"

He groaned. "Don't touch me, I hurt all over; and food would make me sicker."

"I think I should get you to a doctor. I don't want you dying on me," Howy said, popping open one of the cans of sausages.

"You'd have to carry me in, giving the girls a chance to escape."

Howy laughed. "They've already fled."

"When?" Glen yelled, as he struggled to look out the back window.

CHAPTER THIRTY

Hawkman yawned as he parked in front of Harmon's place; a couple more hours of sleep would have helped, but he certainly didn't want to miss this adventure. Trotting up the stairs, he noticed the dogs weren't there; probably hunting. A delicious aroma rushed through the partially opened door. Hawkman knocked on the jamb, then stuck his head inside. "Hey, what's cooking?"

"Hello, Agent Casey, I figured you'd be here right on the nose." He glanced at the battery operated clock sitting on the stove. "In fact, you're one minute early."

It stunned Hawkman when Harmon called him Agent Casey, but he decided to let it pass; maybe he'd find out what Harmon knew before the day ended. "You have quite a feast cooking. Where'd the bacon and eggs come from?"

"Smokehouse and a lady who has more chickens laying than she can use." Harmon pointed to the cabinets on the wall. "Grab us a plate."

Harmon poured the grease into a container, then slapped slices of bread into the skillet and made toast.

While enjoying their meal, they talked about Annie and Babs.

"Where do you think these two thugs have taken the girls?" Harmon asked.

"From the last report I received from Detective Chandler, I'm surmising they've left Happy Camp and going south on Highway 96. It's hard to know if they have a destination."

"I'd bet they're running to lose the police, and are planning to use the women for hostages" Harmon said.

After the two men ate, Hawkman rubbed his stomach. "Food fit for a king. Thank you."

"You're more than welcome. Just drop your plate in the bucket in the sink. We should get on our way and see if we can catch those two thugs."

The men went out the front and trooped down the stairs.

"Where are your dogs?" Hawkman asked.

"They're hunting or romping in the woods."

Hawkman stood back a moment and scrutinized the helicopter. "This is quite a machine. How'd you come by it?"

"I ordered it."

Hawkman waited for more explanation, but Harmon didn't offer any. Puzzled by the man's tight lips, he climbed aboard, fastened the tether, and put on the communication headgear.

Harmon started the rotors and the aircraft lifted smoothly into the air. Hawkman watched him maneuver the controls as they swung over the house. This man is no slouch, Hawkman thought. as they flew toward Highway 96.

***

Howy rolled down his window as the stench coming from Glen's body smelled like rotting flesh and made him nauseated.

He glanced over at his friend, sprawled on the seat with his tee shirt pulled up above his belly button. He noticed the money belt Glen had around his waist.

"Glen, can you hear me?"

"Yeah."

"You look like death warmed over. I'm keeping my eye out for a hospital, but the towns are just not big enough to support one. I'm going to have to get gas soon. I'll ask the station attendant about a clinic or doctor nearby."

Glen moaned. "You're right. I'm really sick."

"If I do find one, you're going to have to shed that money belt. No need for someone to discover you're carrying thousands of dollars. You also need clean clothes, at least a tee shirt. You stink like holy hell."

"Have you spotted Annie and Babs?"

"No, and I don't expect to. So forget about them, they'll probably get lost in this God forsaken country. Right now I'm concentrating on getting into a city with more than a main street, big enough we could get lost in. We need to pick up a used car and abandon this green gas hog which stands out like a sore thumb. Every cop in the county is looking for this rattle trap."

"It got us out of a mess, and has carried us this far," Glen mumbled. "We can be thankful the old fellow took good care of it."

Glen tried to change positions and let out an agonizing cry. He couldn't move his left arm; the pain was so excruciating he fell against the passenger door on his right side, jarring his whole body. His teeth began chattering, and he pulled the bed roll over himself. "I'm freezing."

"You're running a high fever," Howy said. "I can feel the heat radiating off you."

"If I could get my hands on the little brat who stuck me, I'd kill her."

"We'll probably never see them again. Instead of worrying about Annie and Babs, think about a believable story you're going to have to tell a doctor. If they suspect you were knifed, they'll have to report it to the police, and where will that leave us?"

Glen moaned.

"Up ahead is a small town called Somes Bar. I'll fill up, maybe find a doctor, and hopefully, a general store where I can buy some clean clothes for us both."

Howy pulled into the gas station and jumped out of the pickup. He read on the pump he had to pay first; pulling some bills out of his pocket, he went inside. After he paid the cashier, he started to leave, then turned around. "By the way, is there a hospital nearby?"

"The nearest one is about forty miles away," the young woman said.

"Is there a doctor in town?"

"Have you got a problem?" she asked.

"It's not me, but my friend in the truck is running a high fever, and I thought I'd better get him checked out before we go any farther on our trip."

"Yes, there's a doctor in town, Dr. Fredrickson." She jotted down his address on a piece of paper, and checked her watch. "He's probably still in his office." She then told Howy how to get there.

"Is there a general store?"

"Yes, you'll see it on the way to the doctor's."

"Thank you, ma'am. Appreciate your help."

He filled the truck with gas, then drove down the highway to the turnoff the cashier had told him to take. The big mercantile couldn't be missed with a huge red banner, advertising a sale, draped across the front. Howy pulled into the lot and found a big shade tree to park under.

"Glen, what size jeans and shirt do you wear?"

He tried to get his eyes open a slit, and quickly told Howy his sizes.

"I'll hurry," Howy said. "Roll down the window if you get too hot. I've also found a doctor."

"Thanks." Glen then pulled the bed roll over his shoulder.

Howy rushed into the huge barn like building, and had no problem spotting the items he needed. He purchased the clothing and high tailed it back to the truck. The parking lot was almost empty, so he figured this was as good a place as any to get Glen's fresh clothes on. Too bad he had to pull them over such a filthy body. He hopped into the cab.

"Okay, Glen, I'm going to need your help."

They were able to manuever the underwear and jeans on without too much difficulty, but Howy could see the shirt was going to be a hassle. No way could he get the bloody tee off by pulling it over Glen's head.

"I'm going to have to cut your shirt off. I bought a soft flannel one that buttons down the front, plus a new tee. We'll just work with the flannel."

Howy took his pocket knife and slowly ripped the shirt up the back. He had no trouble with removing the right side, but on the left side, blood and pus had soaked through the bandage and stuck to the cloth.

"Man, this looks bad. I'm not going to try and get it off, I'll let the doc do it. Whew, and it stinks." Howy took the money belt and put it around his waist. "I'll wear this until you feel up to it; don't want to leave it in the truck."

Finally, after getting Glen dressed, Howy quickly changed and threw all the filthy clothes behind the seat. He'd take care of those later. Right now he wanted to find the doctor's office.

He followed the woman's instructions, which led him into a residential area. He drove up and down the street. Almost ready to give up, when he spotted the mailbox at the curb with the name, Dr. Fredrickson, in black block letters painted on the side. Howy glanced at the small house, and a shingle hung from the porch. He turned into the driveway, which led to a parking lot for about five cars. A big oak tree shaded the space.

Howy helped his friend from the truck and Glen's knees almost buckled due to his weakness. Howy had to practically carry him into the office. When the nurse-receptionist glanced up, she jumped from her seat and started to take ahold of Glen's left side, but Howy stopped her.

"Don't touch him there, he's got a terrible infection and he screams if it gets touched."

"Oh, my goodness, what happened?" she asked.

Knowing what Glen had planned to tell the doctor, Howy said, "He fell."

"Let's get him into a patient waiting room, and I'll summon the doctor right away."

When they got Glen situated, she carefully removed his shirt, and made a face. "Oh, dear, this is bad."

CHAPTER THIRTY-ONE

Annie moaned, rolled over, and sat up. She shaded her eyes and looked skyward as she heard the unmistakable sound of a helicopter. "You hear that, Babs?"

"Yes, but I don't see it."

"Me, either. Could be a police or traffic craft."

"Should we try to signal to it?"

Annie stood and looked down the road. "Looks like the copter just passed us."

"So much for that thought." Babs brushed off her clothes. "I feel like there's a million small pebbles embedded into my body."

"Sleeping on the ground will do it every time," Annie said, smiling.

Babs got to her feet and stretched, followed by Lucy, who shook the dirt from her coat.

"Oh, Lucy, now I've got dust up my nose," Babs said, letting loose with a couple of sneezes.

"Are you hungry?" Annie asked.

Babs shook her head. "Not yet, but I'll haul the backpack. You've carried it long enough."

"It's not very heavy; only a few cans left," Annie said.

Babs pulled the straps over her shoulders. "Are we ready to continue our trek?"

"Yep, let's hit the road, or I should say, dirt. How sweet it will be to shed these dirty clothes and take a soak in a bathtub."

Babs laughed. "I never thought I'd see the day I'd look forward to a good scrubbing." She sniffed under her arm. "Phew, I've got B.O."

They both giggled as they hiked north, staying a few yards from the edge of the highway so they wouldn't be seen by the traffic.

***

Harmon flew over Highway 96, while Hawkman examined the vehicles with binoculars.

"Pay close attention to the pickups, as we've just passed Happy Camp. Detective Chandler said the campsites had already been checked for the criminals, so more than likely they've headed south. I see no reason for them to turn around." Harmon said.

"Me, either. If my memory serves me right, there are not many side roads."

"Correct, and they wouldn't want to drive into a barren area where they couldn't get gas or food. There's a little town a few miles down called Somes Bar, and it has a gas station on the outskirts. I'll set down nearby and we can talk to the attendant."

"Sounds like you've done this before."

A grin quivered at the edges of Harmon's mouth. "I have."

Hawkman went back to monitoring the vehicles on the highway. He knew this wasn't the time to probe the pilot, but sensed the man had enjoyed having fun with him.

Harmon pulled the copter up several times to avoid hitting the sides of the hills with the rotor blades when the passage became narrow. Soon, he pointed ahead. "We're coming into Somes Bar; there's the gas station."

He dropped the helicopter down and landed it softly on an even spot next to the building; not even a bounce. Once Harmon cut off the power, the blades slowed to a stop; the men removed their headgear, then jumped out of the cockpit.

Harmon went straight to the door and stepped inside. "Hello, Miss Jane."

She glanced up with a big grin, then hopped off the tall stool behind the counter. Standing on her tiptoes, she threw her arms around his neck and gave him a big kiss on the cheek.

"It's so good to see you. How have you been?" she asked.

"I wanted to say the same thing to you, but you beat me to it," he said.

"I have a feeling this is not a social trip," she said, glancing at Hawkman.

"No, we're on a mission and hoped you could help us."

"I'll certainly try."

"Have you recently served a 1973 faded green Chevy pickup?"

"Yes, just this morning."

"Were there two men, two women and a dog in the truck?"

She tapped her chin. "I only talked to the man who came in and paid for the gas. Let me ask my assistant."

She stepped to the door. "Jason," she called, motioning for him to come inside.

He hurried and moved into the room. "Yes, Miss Jane."

She asked him about the occupants of the vehicle.

"Only two men, the one driving and a very sick passenger."

"How did you know he was ill?" Harmon asked.

"I got a good look at him while cleaning the windshield. He had a flushed face and shivered so hard I could see him shaking, even with a sleeping bag wrapped around him."

Hawkman pulled out the sketches he had in his pocket. "Do these men look familiar?"

Casey nodded and pointed to Glen. "This guy had the tremors."

Miss Jane looked at the pictures, and gestured toward Howy. "He asked me about a General Store and a hospital. When I told him we didn't have a medical center nearby, he asked if I knew a doctor; I gave him Dr. Fredrickson's office address." She looked up at Harmon. "Why are you searching for these two?"

"They're bank robbers and kidnappers. They took two women and their dog as hostages. Now we're worried about what's happened to the two females and their pet."

"Oh, dear, this could turn dreadful," Miss Jane said.

"Is there some way we could get this Dr. Fredrickson to drop by here?" Hawkman asked.

"I can certainly give him a call," Miss Jane said. "I hope he's still at the office. This is not the busiest place around," she smiled, as she picked up the phone.

To give Miss Jane some privacy, Harmon and Hawkman walked around the small enclosure, examining the old time ads hanging on the walls, along with pictures of former owners.

"He'll be right over. I caught him just in time," she said, hanging up the phone.

"Thank you," Hawkman said.

The two men walked outside into the warm spring day, went to the soda dispenser and bought a Coke. Each were sipping on the cool drinks when a CTS bronze Cadillac drove up, and parked at the side of the building. The doctor, still in his white coat, climbed out of the car. A distinguished looking man, in his late forties, tall and slim with graying temples, approached them. He held out his hand to Harmon.

"Hello, Harmon, long time since I've seen you."

The two men shook hands. "I'd like you to meet Private Investigator, Tom Casey," Harmon said

After the introductions, the three sat on wooden chairs on the small porch.

Hawkman brought out the sketches of Howy and Glen. "Did you by any chance treat one of these men today?"

The doctor slipped on a pair of glasses and studied the papers. "Yes, both were in my office, but this one," he pointed to Glen, "turned out to be very sick. An injury he'd received, which he told me had occurred during a fall, had become horribly infected. I truly don't believe he got it from falling down an embankment while hiking. In my opinion, it looked like a knife wound he'd had for several days. His body smelled to high heaven; I doubt he'd bathed in quite a few days. He had on a new shirt, but part of the old one stuck on the wound and my assistant had a time getting it off. So, why are you interested in these men?"

Hawkman told him the history, then inquired about the two women. "Did either of them mention an Annie or Babs?"

The doctor shook his head. "I can't even tell you either of their last names, as they paid cash for my services. The fellow who brought the skinny one in, introduced himself as Howy and his pal, Glen. Said they were on vacation and hiking in different areas when the unfortunate incident happened. I told him I'd like to see Glen in a couple of days, as blood poisoning could set in and I wanted to make sure we curbed it. However, I doubt I'll ever see either of them again."

Hawkman handed the doctor a business card. "If you do, please call this number, it will find me."

He stuck it in his pocket. "I certainly will."

CHAPTER THIRTY-TWO

While Howy sat in the waiting room, he'd asked the assistant about a motel nearby. She directed him to a group of cabins about five miles down the road, tucked away in the forest, so he had to watch the signs or he'd miss the turnoff. It sounded like a perfect spot for him and Glen to get a good night's rest, not to mention a place to clean up.

Howy practically carried Glen to the pickup. The doctor had given him a tranquilizer, plus medication to deaden the pain while he scraped and cleaned the wound, then sewed it up. After the doc finished, he'd handed Howy a bottle of antibiotics and pain killers. He said he wanted to see Glen again, but no way would that happen; they had to get out of there before someone got wise.

Driving down the highway, Howy spotted the sign 'Jenny's Cabins' and slowed. Arrows pointed the way. He decided to check them out before renting one for the night. Driving down to the last cabin, he liked what he saw, turned around and headed back to the building that had the word 'Office' on the front door.

Glen hadn't moved and appeared in a deep sleep, resting peacefully. Howy removed a roll of bills from Glen's money belt, stuck it in his pocket, locked the driver's side door, and strolled to the head cabin. A sign said to 'ring bell', which he did. Within a few minutes, a young woman in her early thirties, with shiny black hair that hung to her waist, opened the door. Her almost black eyes sparkled as she stared into his face. Her smooth silken skin, glowing like a diamond, covered high cheek bones. It took Howy back as he'd never seen such a beautiful woman. Then he noticed she only had one arm, and supported herself with a crutch as one leg appeared shorter than the other.

"Hello, may I help you?" she asked.

"Uh, yes. I-I'd like to rent a cabin," he stuttered.

"Of course, please come in."

When he entered, he spotted a huge German Shepherd sitting in front of the fireplace, who didn't take his gaze off of him. As the woman walked around a tall counter, he noticed her body bent over in an odd sort of way; she'd been in a horrible accident, or born that way. Resting her crutch on the wood, she shuffled a small pad of paper to the front, and asked him a few questions, then wrote down the answers. After she told Howy the price, he pulled the roll of money from his pocket, peeled off the bills and placed them on the countertop.

She reached under the wood and brought out a set of keys. "Your cabin is number four. It has two beds as you requested and is situated straight down this side of the road; the number is on a plaque out front. You can't miss it." She wrote out a receipt and handed it to him. "Thank you, so much."

He nodded, and left the cabin with the vision of her beautiful face still swimming in his mind. Glancing inside the pickup before unlocking it, he was relieved to see Glen still asleep and hadn't moved. He climbed in, drove down to their cabin and parked as close to the front door as he could. Hauling Glen in and out of the pickup had worn him to a frazzle.

Howy hopped out of the truck, stepped onto the porch of the small abode, unlocked the door and pushed it open. His chin dropped. He did not expect such a stunning place. Two oak queen size beds sat in the middle of the room, with what looked like homemade crocheted spreads. A big screen television sat on a huge table. Pictures of gold mines, Indians and trains littered the walls. All the chairs were carved from beautiful oak, with big pillow embroidered seats. The place appeared more like a home, than a place for travelers.

He pulled back the covers on one of the beds, then went back out to the truck to get Glen. He tried to wake him, to no avail, and finally picked him up, being careful of his left side. Glen ended up hanging over Howy's shoulder like a limp noodle; but finally, he got him inside and into the bed. At least the fever had broke and his natural color had returned to his face.

Panting, Howy returned to the truck and moved it behind the cabin, under the shade of the trees, so it couldn't be seen from the main road. Back in the cabin, he locked the door, checked on Glen, then headed for the shower.

He couldn't believe he could actually see the dirt from his body flowing down the drain. No wonder the stab wound on Glen's shoulder got infected. Howy decided to let his beard grow, even though a disposable razor lay on the counter. Maybe it would disguise his looks. He slipped on the new clothes he'd bought; even though worn for a day, they were better than what he'd thrown behind the pickup seat. He felt refreshed when he came back into the main room, but very hungry.

All of a sudden Glen sat straight up. "Where the hell are we?"

"Calm down. We're in a fancy cabin tucked away in the forest and away from the highway. I figured we needed a good night's rest and a bath."

"Where are Annie and Babs?"

"I already told you, they escaped."

Glen tossed back the covers and threw his legs over the edge of the bed. "Well, we gotta find 'em."

"Not tonight. We're not going anywhere. If I were you, I wouldn't move too quickly. The
doc filled you with all kinds of drugs."

Glen tried to stand up, but fell back on the bed. "Whew, I think you're right. My head is whirling and I feels like I'm floating."

Howy removed the two medicine bottles from his shirt pocket and handed them to his friend. "The doc gave you these. You're due for a dose of antibiotic; the you only take the pain killers when needed."

Glen set the bottles on the bed stand. "Would you mind getting me a glass of water?"

Howy rolled his eyes and reluctantly brought him the water. "I'm going to call for a pizza delivery, I'm starving."

"Me, too."

Howy went to the phone and found several brochures tucked underneath the base showing places that would deliver. He made a selection and put in the order. Sitting down on his bed, he stared at Glen. "Why did you say we have to find Annie and Babs?"

"Because the little brat has put me through misery, and she can't go on thinking she got by with it. She has to be taught a lesson."

"Of course, robbing a bank is okay?"

"It's different. Nobody got hurt."

"That's a matter of opinion. What about the people who lost their life's savings?"

"I'm sure the bank had some sort of insurance. Anyway, what's with you? You going soft on me?"

"No, just wondered what you had in mind."

Someone knocked, and Howy fingered the gun stowed in his pocket. "Who's there?"

"Pizza delivery."

"Okay, coming."

He opened the door a few inches, looked out, then released the chain. Taking the two large boxes and soft drinks, he paid the boy with a hefty tip, then locked and chained the door.

"Oh, man this smells so good," Howy said, handing Glen a drink and a pizza.

They both chowed down, and didn't let up until the last piece of crust had disappeared.

"I think I'm going to live now," Glen said, letting out a huge burp. "Damn, just got my belly full, and my shoulder is starting to hurt like hell."

"What'd you do with the pain pills?"

Glen picked up the bottles. "Ah, my salvation." He threw one into his mouth, and washed it down with his soda.

"Before it knocks you out, you were going to tell me what you had in mind for Annie and Babs."

"You sure you want to know?"

"Yes."

"I plan to rape the mom, then kill the kid and her dog."

CHAPTER THIRTY-THREE

Howy frowned. "I don't cherish the thought of being an accomplice to murder. If we get caught for the armed robbery, we could be spending twenty years in jail. Add murder and they'll throw away the key."

"So you don't like my plan?"

"Not at all."

"Okay, we'll make a deal. You keep the brat and her dog away from me while I have my way with her mother."

"The pain killer must be affecting your brain. You're really talking crazy. For one thing, we don't even know where they are."

"If they got away while you were sleeping, they're on foot. We'll find them."

"They could have hitched a ride back to their home."

When Howy didn't receive a response, he glanced at Glen to see his chin had drifted down against his chest and he'd fallen asleep.

***

Harmon extended his hand. "Thank you, Dr. Fredrickson, for going out of your way to give us this information."

"No problem. I just hope it helps."

"It has, and we really appreciate it," Hawkman said, shaking the doctor's hand.

The physician drove away, and Harmon stuck his head in the door of the gas station to tell Miss Jane goodbye. She waved at Casey, then the two men took off in the helicopter.

"Who stabbed Glen?" Harmon said, speaking into the tiny microphone of the headgear.

Hawkman shook his head. "Annie or Babs are feisty enough. Unfortunately, if one of them did, we might find their bodies in a shallow grave."

Harmon grimaced. "I'm going to take another run south on Highway 96. If Glen is as sick as Dr. Fredrickson said, they may have stopped off the road. We'll be able to spot Ed's truck."

Harmon pulled the air craft around and flew down the corridor just above the traffic. Hawkman had the binoculars glued to his face, checking every side road and vehicle they passed. Finally, Harmon turned the copter north, and surveyed the area again, in case they'd missed something.

Letting the binoculars rest on his chest, Hawkman removed his hat and wiped his forehead. "They're here somewhere. I can feel it in my gut. Maybe we should go back to your place and get the 4X4. They could be parked in a grove of trees and we'd never see the truck from up here."

"I hear ya," Harmon said. "I'm also getting low on fuel."

"Where do you get it?"

"I have a tank at my place. Once a month a guy comes out and tops it off for me."

"Harmon, you amaze me. When I first met you, I thought you were as poor as a church mouse, but obviously, you're not. Here you are sporting a helicopter, fuel to feed it, and a generator in your basement. I certainly wouldn't call that destitute. What surprises me is you don't have some sort of vehicle to get you around."

Harmon threw back his head and laughed. "Oh, but I do, it's in the garage."

Hawkman furrowed his brow. "I don't remember seeing another building near your house."

"It's underground."

"So it's true what I found out about you? I did some research and found out your name is Ronald Getty and you're an undercover man."

Mr. Getty grinned. "Do you think I'd be telling you all this stuff if I hadn't done a search on you?"

"Oh, yeah? What'd you find out?"

"Well, after talking with Mr. Broadwell, your old boss, I decided we were comrades. Your birth name is Jim Anderson, which had to be changed to Tom Casey, when your life became in danger. You married the classy little widow on the other side of Lake Copco. I believe her name is Jennifer. You have an adopted son, Sam. Need I say any more? I can go on and on."

Hawkman chuckled. "Don't think it's necessary. It's good working with you. I can see why you're so interested in getting Annie and Babs back safely. Your job is embedded in your soul, just like me. Except you're still working with the Agency. I'm retired, and have taken on the new handle of private investigator."

"Damn good one too."

"Thanks."

Harmon curved around the side of the house and set the aircraft down without so much as a bump.

"You want me to help you get it under the house?" Hawkman asked as they climbed out of the cockpit.

"No, we might need it later. We'll just tie it down."

They soon had the helicopter secure, headed to the front of the house and hopped into Hawkman's 4X4. Before long, they were cruising south on Highway 96. They'd just passed Happy Camp when up ahead they saw a barricade across the road with red blinking lights and warning cones.

"What the heck?" Harmon said, as the traffic came to a halt.

A patrolman directed vehicles to make U-turns. Hawkman stuck his head out the window. "What's happened, Officer?"

"Bad wreck up ahead. Big rig and several cars; injuries involved. It'll be several hours before the road is clear. We're advising people to turn around and wait until morning before coming this way. We're working on getting the road closed before people get this far."

Hawkman turned around and headed back to Harmon's place. "It seems we're getting delayed every time we think we've got a bead on these guys."

"Maybe it will turn out for the best. They'll relax, thinking they've made it to safety; and that's when they'll make a mistake," Harmon said.

"I hope you're right, but they're bound to know the cops are looking for Ed's stolen truck, and the two women."

"Once they get out of this area, those reports are put on the back burner. Each town has its own priorities."

"The thing that bothers me the most, is the attendant at the gas station who said there were just the two men. Where were Annie and Babs?" Hawkman asked.

"It disturbs me, too. However, the thought crossed my mind; they just might have escaped."

"How? Where the hell could they go without those guys catching them again."

Harmon shook his head. "There could have been an opportunity when Glen was suffering with an infection setting in. Howy would have to get some rest along the way, and Glen could have passed out with a high fever. I know it sounds like a long shot, but it's definitely possible."

Hawkman pulled up in front of Harmon's place. "Shall we go searching early tomorrow morning? Hopefully, they'll have the road open."

"Sounds like a good plan. I'll be ready at six."

Harmon hopped out of the 4X4. The bloodhounds greeted him with their howls of happiness as he jogged up the stairs.

Hawkman soon pulled into his garage; with a growling stomach, he strolled into the kitchen.

Jennifer glanced up at him as he put his arms around her waist.

"That sure smells good," he said.

"Have you not eaten all day?"

"Nope, think I'll take some sandwiches tomorrow."

"Sounds like you didn't have any luck today."

"Mother luck did not smile on us at all. Even the road crews had it out for us."

"Wash up and I'll fill our plates, then you can tell me all about it."

CHAPTER THIRTY-FOUR

Annie and Babs wove around the trees, climbed over fallen logs and pushed through heavy brush as they continued their journey toward Happy Camp. Lucy, with her nose to the ground, followed closely behind the two.

Suddenly, Babs took a tumble and cried out in pain. Annie ran to her side, and bent over her fallen body.

"Are you okay?"

Tears welled in Babs eyes. "No, I think I've really broken my ankle this time."

Annie shoved the bushes aside and saw where Babs' foot had wedged between two big limbs. She carefully moved the branches and gently lifted her daughter's leg.

Babs gritted her teeth, put hands over her face and let out a groan. "Oh, it hurts."

Annie grimaced as she eyed the child's ankle. It hung at a strange angle. "You've definitely done some damage. This may be painful, but I'm going to try to elevate it."

Tears ran down Babs' face as she tried not to scream when her mother worked to get a couple of logs, one on top of the other, to hold firm. Once she had them in place, she carefully put

Babs' leg on them. "This should help relieve some of the pain. Try to relax, if you can."

Lucy moved to her owner's side and whined as she placed her head on Babs' stomach.

Babs put her hand on her pet's neck. "What are we going to do?"

Annie sighed. "I don't know. I can't leave you in this condition, and you're too heavy for me to carry. We'll have to think about our next move." Annie sat down Indian style beside her daughter's shoulder, and brushed tangled hair off her closed eyes. "Are you feeling less discomfort with the leg up?"

Babs nodded. "These are the times when it would be nice to have enough money to have a cell phone."

Annie smiled in spite of their dilemma. "You're right, but it would've been taken away from us at the beginning of this debacle."

"Guess I should be happy we're alive."

Taking a deep breath, Annie stood, brushed off her butt, and meandered toward the highway until she could see the pavement. She stayed hidden, but frowned, wondering why no vehicles were in sight. Then she heard a siren and ducked behind a tree. She watched an ambulance race by; then another speeding in the opposite direction. "Uh, oh," she mumbled. "Bet there's been a bad accident and they have the road blocked."

She turned and strolled back to where Babs lay on the ground. Fortunately, they were in a sheltered area, as Annie had noticed how breezy and cool it had become. Glancing at Babs' ankle, she frowned, and bent down to loosen the shoe laces. The ankle had really swollen, and she knew Babs needed to get to a doctor. She might have to take the chance and leave her to go seek help.

Lucy would stay with her and defend Babs against any wild animals, all except the two legged creatures who carried guns. Annie sucked in her breath, leaned back against a tree trunk and closed her eyes.

Jolted from a light sleep, Annie heard a voice calling.

"Mom, Mom."

Not being used to hearing Babs voice, it took her a minute to realize her daughter had broken the silence and needed her. She rose from her position and stumbled toward the mound on the ground.

"Are you in pain?"

"Not bad, as long as I don't move. I think you should leave me and Lucy here; and you go find help." Babs dug into the pocket of her jeans. "Also, here's one of my pocket knives; you might need it. I have another, so don't worry."

Annie stuck the knife in her pocket. "I've already decided I need to go for help, but not until morning. Let's eat a bite before it's too dark to see."

Annie dragged the backpack around Babs' head from where she'd dropped it when she fell. Peering into the bag, Annie searched around and brought out some cans. "We're in luck, there's a total of six left; should get us by for another day." She held up each can so she could see the labels. "Madam, which gourmet tidbit would you like tonight?" Reading them off in an uppity voice, she had Babs laughing.

They made their picks; Babs fed Lucy, then the three huddled together to try to sleep. The night had turned quite chilly and Annie pulled up the sweatshirt hood and tied it under her chin to keep her ears warm. She helped Babs do the same. Soon, they all drifted into sleep.

***

When Howy finally turned off the lights and his head hit the pillow, he immediately fell into a deep sleep. Several times during the night Glen yelled for him to shut up and turn over.

Morning soon arrived, and Howy bounded out of bed and headed for the phone where he ordered pancakes and ham for two. He glanced at the bed and his mouth dropped open. Glen wasn't there. He hung up and called his name; a weak answer came from the bathroom. Howy dashed to the room, where he found Glen in the bathtub.

"You better not get your wound wet; could cause a problem," Howy scolded

"Hey, do I have stupid written across my forehead? Why do you think I'm in the tub and not taking a shower."

"The way the medications have affected you, I didn't know for sure. I'm glad you're bathing. I don't think I could have stood riding with you another day."

"You can leave now and let me finish up."

"Breakfast has been ordered, so don't soak too long."

Howy left the bathroom area, and heard the knock at the door.

"Who's there," he called, fingering the pistol in his pocket.

"Breakfast."

He paid for the food, then carried it to the table in the kitchenette. Glen came out dressed, his hair combed and smelling better than Howy ever remembered. After they downed the pancakes, Glen stood.

"Okay, let's get on the road."

"Are you still serious about finding Annie and Babs?" Howy asked.

"You damned right. I'll follow those two back to their house to get my revenge. My shoulder will never be the same and she's going to pay for it."

Howy sighed. "Aren't you carrying this a bit too far? She was only trying to protect her mother."

Glen put his fist on his hip, narrowed his eyes and glared at Howy. "It ain't like she was a virgin."

Changing the subject, Howy shifted his position. "We'll really be asking for trouble if we head back into their territory with that truck. Every police officer will be looking for it and we certainly can't outrun any of their cars. Next thing we know, we'll be headed for the clunker."

Glen flopped down in the overstuffed chair in the corner and winced as his shoulder met with the rough fabric. He immediately came forward. "I've been thinking about getting a different vehicle."

"How do you plan to find it?"

"We've got enough money to buy one at a used car lot. If we stole one out of a parking lot, the cops would be on our tails."

"Good point, unless the owner of the lot saw our pictures and got suspicious."

Glen waved a hand. "Most of those guys are crooks. They're just interested in their profit; they don't care who buys, as long as they see the green stuff."

"I agree, but we're in the boonies. Where the hell are we going to find a used car lot?" Then he snapped his fingers. "Stay here for a few minutes, let me go talk to the girl running these cabins.

She seems knowledgeable about the area and will know where we can find one."

"Go for it," Glen said, not moving from the chair.

CHAPTER THIRTY-FIVE

Howy smiled to himself as he strolled toward the office. He didn't want Glen to see the beautiful girl. He'd only make some comment about her handicap and probably want to rape her. Howy just wanted to look upon her loveliness and continue his dreams.

He rapped lightly on the door, in hopes she'd awakened and dressed for the day. Since she seemed to be in charge, he assumed she'd be up. She opened the door and smiled.

"Is everything all right?" she asked, with a flitting frown.

Howy raised a hand. "Oh, yeah, we're enjoying the cabin. I wanted to ask if you knew where I could find a used car lot."

"Is there something wrong with your vehicle?"

Howy rocked back on his heels. "Not really. I know this is going to sound lame, but my friend got hurt in an accident and the truck is so rough he's really uncomfortable. We still have many miles to go, so thought we'd just get a car; they ride a lot smoother."

"Did you plan to trade in the pickup?"

"No, I can't, because it's my uncle's and I'll have to find a place to store it until he can come for it."

"I might be able to save you some time, if you'd be interested in a perfect, well maintained, eight year old Cadillac Seville, driven only 75,000 miles."

Howy's eyes widened. "Sounds just like what we're looking for. Where would I find this dream machine?"

"Follow me," she said. Taking her cane, she stepped out the front door and moved to the tall fence at the side of the house. Opening a wide gate; she motioned him through.

Howy's mouth dropped open as he eyed the pristine silver colored Cadillac. "This your car?"

"Yes, I have a new one ordered."

Figuring she wanted a steep price, he shaded his eyes and peered inside at the immaculate interior. "How much are you asking?"

"I'd like to get seven thousand."

"Is that your bottom price?"

She grinned. "It is, if you want me to store your uncle's truck until he can pick it up."

Howy chuckled. "You drive a hard bargain. Mind if I check under the hood?"

"Not at all."

He couldn't believe how new the engine looked. She'd obviously had it steamed cleaned. "You certainly took good care of this vehicle."

"Thank you. It's also full of gas, and for a big car it gets very good mileage."

"May I start it up?"

"Certainly." She pulled a set of keys out of her pocket and handed them to him.

The engine turned over on the first try, and hummed like a baby.

"Lady, you just made yourself a deal. I'll be right back with the money."

"Drive it up to your cabin and show your friend. Then bring down the pickup, and we'll put it in here."

Howy opened up the broad gate, and carefully drove out the car, then headed toward the cabin. He could hardly wait for Glen to see it. When he went inside, his friend still sat in the overstuffed chair, and looked very pale.

"You okay?" Howy asked.

"I'm still not up to par, but I'll be okay. The meds the doc gave me are working; I can tell."

"I've got something to show you, but you'll have to come outside."

"This better be good," Glen said, slowly standing. He put a hand on the wall as he eased to the door. When he looked out, his mouth dropped open. "Where the hell did you get this baby?"

Howy gave him a quick rundown of the transaction. "I need to get the truck and money to her right now."

Howy quickly cleaned out the pickup of their filthy clothes, fast-food containers, and threw them in the nearby dumpster. The two men went inside and divided up the money to pay for the Cadillac. Howy then jumped into the truck and drove it down to Jenny's cabin. He knew he should trust Glen, but he didn't and had slipped the Cadillac keys into his pocket. He hoped Jenny had another set.

Driving the pickup into the slot next to the building, he closed the gate then went inside to the office. They filled out the paperwork and Jenny gave Howy an extra set of keys.

"Thanks so much," she said, walking him to the door. "Have your uncle call me the day he wants to pick up his truck, to make sure I'll be here. My number is on the card I gave you."

"Will do," Howy said, as he left her abode.

Howy jogged back to the cabin, thrilled with the new car. No one would know them, and the pickup was hidden behind a tall fence. "Life is good," he mumbled.

When he stepped into their cottage, he did a double take. Glen had sprawled out on the bed and appeared asleep.

"Hey, Glen, what's with you? I thought you were gung ho to go?"

"I am, man, but I'm still sick."

"You want me to rent the cabin for another day?"

"Right now I'm in no shape to be running after Annie and Babs. Maybe another good night's rest will do the trick."

Howy fished out the amount of money needed for another night from their money belts, and went out the door.

***

Glen adjusted the cloth sling the doctor had given him to hold his shoulder still while it healed. Then he lay down and bunched the pillows under his head, but in doing so he shoved them too hard and the corner hit his wound. He gritted his teeth. "Shit, that hurt. Damn Babs, she's going to pay for what she did to me. My shoulder will never move the same way, and will probably give me fits for the rest of my life," he said out loud. Then an evil grin appeared on his mouth. "Her momma will make every thing right."

The pain killer he'd taken a few minutes ago started to work and he grew drowsy. His thoughts went to Howy. He didn't really like him, but what in the world would he have done without his help? If the situation had been in reverse, he knew he didn't have the patience Howy had shown. He'd have shoved him out of the truck, and left the man in the woods where he would've died.

Howy came in the door about the time he had these morbid thoughts and it made him feel a little bit guilty. "What the hell are you carrying?"

"She wanted us to move to a clean cabin, but I told her we'd rather stay where we are, if possible; and we didn't need any housecleaning, so she gave me fresh towels, linens, bar soap, shampoo, and I'm not sure what else."

"Nice lady."

"Yeah, she is," Howy said, as he placed the stack of stuff on a small table in the corner.

"This is really a neat place," Glen said. "You sure we can't be seen from the highway?"

"Positive; and the old truck is behind a tall solid wood fence. I'll show you when we leave out of here tomorrow in the new car." Howy hit his thigh and laughed. "We've got the cops fooled now. They'd never expect us to be in a shiny Cadillac. I'll have to watch my speed; sure don't want to get a ticket at this point."

Glen grinned. "I'll be glad when I can take my turn to drive."

"You sure seem to be in better spirits than an hour ago."

"The painkiller has kicked in. I don't have to take one as often as I did yesterday, so that's a good sign. Take a smooth riding automobile along with a good night's rest, and I'll be ready to hit the road in the morning.

"Yeah, I'm getting a little antsy staying around here for too long. We need to get in a more populated area, instead of these little one-horse towns, so we can get lost in a crowd."

CHAPTER THIRTY-SIX

Sitting at the kitchen bar after eating, Hawkman told Jennifer about how he and Harmon had run into bad luck the whole day. When he told about the gas station where the robbers had stopped to fill the tank, and the women were not with them, Jennifer frowned.

"This doesn't sound good," she said.

Hawkman nodded. "I know, but we can't give up hope. Harmon and I are taking off early in the morning to do some more searching. Annie and Babs could have somehow escaped the men and are wandering around in the hills. I doubt they'd be near the highway, afraid the robbers will be looking for them. Hopefully, they've headed toward home."

"Are you going in Harmon's helicopter?" she asked.

"No, we decided to take my 4X4; easier to stop at places and ask questions."

"If the girls aren't near the main road, how do you expect to find them?"

"We need to get some sort of clue to find out if they're still with the two men."

"You just said the two criminals were seen at a gas station without them."

Hawkman raised his brows and glared at his wife. "You're driving me crazy with all these questions."

She ducked her head. "Sorry, I'm just so concerned about Annie and Babs. I feel so helpless."

He reached over and patted her hand. "It's okay. My nerves are on edge because I feel they're a step ahead and we can't reach them. As far as your question goes, Howy and Glen could have tied the girls up and left them somewhere when they went to get gas."

Jennifer shrugged. "Guess that's possible, but doesn't sound feasible."

"I'd rather think positive," Hawkman said, yawning and stretching his arms above his head. "I'm hitting the sack; got another early morning tomorrow."

***

Hawkman arose before the sun; clothes thrown over his arm and boots in his hand, he tiptoed out of the bedroom. Flipping on the heat to kill the morning chill, he dressed in the guest bathroom. On his way into the kitchen, he filled Miss Marple's food bowl, in hopes the feline wouldn't wake Jennifer. Then he put on a pot of coffee.

While the coffee perked, he had a bowl of dry cereal and a cup of yogurt. Once the java had brewed, he poured himself a mug and put the rest into a thermos. He punched the garage door opener he had on the window sill and watched the big door slowly open. He left through the entry, making sure Miss Marple didn't try to slip out, then quietly closed it.

As he approached Harmon's place, Hawkman spotted him standing at the end of his driveway. He pulled to a stop, and Harmon climbed aboard.

"You're two minutes late," Harmon said, with a grin.

Hawkman chuckled. "I had to stop for some cows crossing the road."

"Good excuse; you're forgiven."

"I've been thinking about where we should go to continue our search. How does heading south on Highway 96 to Somes Bar sound?" Hawkman asked.

"Excellent choice. We know the two men have traveled that road, and we need to stop at a few places to ask if they've been seen."

As they drove south, the sun traveled higher in the sky and the day warmed. About eight thirty, Hawkman's cell phone rang. He punched it on, using the hands free equipment.

"Tom Casey, here"

"Mr. Casey, this is Dr. Fredrickson."

Hawkman glanced at Harmon.

"Yes, what can I do for you?"

"I just found out some information you might be interested in hearing."

"I'm listening."

"Before I go into it, have Howy and Glen been caught yet?"

"No."

"I hope this helps. When I told my receptionist that Howy and Glen were two con men, she informed me that while I worked on Glen, and Howy sat in the waiting room, he asked her if there were any motels around. Being innocent of the men's background, she told him about Jenny's Cabins."

"Where are they located?" Hawkman asked.

"About five miles south past Somes Bar on 96. They're off the highway and you can't see them from the road, so you have to keep alert for the signs or you'll miss the turnoff."

"Did your receptionist give him any other suggestions?"

"No, as there are no other overnight places until you get on down the road for several miles."

"Thank you, Dr. Fredrickson, I really appreciate this information."

After hanging up, Hawkman turned to Harmon. "You know this place?"

"I've heard about Jenny's Cabins, but never seen them. I understand they're managed by a beautiful in the face, but severely handicapped young woman. The cabins are reasonably priced, and supposedly works of art."

"There's no question where we're headed. We're about an hour and a half from Somes Bar."

The men rode in silence for about thirty minutes, then Harmon pointed at a car coming from the opposite direction.

"Wow, look at that beautiful silver Cadillac. Showroom classic."

"That is a beauty," Hawkman said, as it passed them.

Soon they reached the outskirts of Somes Bar, drove past the small town and looked for signs to Jenny's Cabins.

"Slow down, it appears the turnoff is up ahead," Harmon said.

Hawkman turned off the highway onto a blacktop road and then made a left as he followed the signs to Jenny's Cabins. He pulled into a well-manicured area, reminding him of a cul-de-sac, with fantasy cabins scattered around the outer edges surrounded by mature trees; a beautiful setting. Stopping in front of the first chalet which had a shingle hanging from the front porch stating 'Office', the two men climbed out and approached the entrance. When they opened the door, a small bell tinkled. Just as they stepped up to the counter, a beautiful young woman, with the use of a cane and only one arm, hobbled from the back. Her shiny black hair hung below her waist and a big smile lit up the room.

"Hello, gentlemen, how may I help you?"

"Are you Ms Jenny, the manager?" Harmon asked.

"Yes, I am."

"My God, you're beautiful," he said.

She ducked her head and blushed. "Thank you. I'm afraid with my other handicaps, it doesn't help much."

Hawkman glanced at Harmon. Knowing he'd lost him, he quickly took out his Private Investigator badge and flashed it. "We're here on official business and would like to ask you some questions."

Her expression completely changed to a frown. "Is something wrong?"

"Not with your business." Hawkman placed the two pictures of Howy and Glen, that Babs had sketched, on the top of the counter. "We just want to know if you recognize either of these men."

Jenny first studied the one of Glen, then put it down and picked up the one of Howy.

"This man rented a cabin for two nights. He just left this morning."

Hawkman pointed at the drawing of Glen. "Are you sure this man wasn't with him?"

She wrinkled her brow. "He said he had a very sick friend with him and wanted a cabin for two, but I never actually saw the person, only a silhouette in the car. So I leased him my number four as it is the roomiest with two queen size beds. I'd show it to you, but it's rented at the moment."

"That wouldn't be necessary, as I doubt we'd find anything to give us a hint of where they went."

"Is there a problem with these two men?"

Hawkman gave her a quick rundown on the antics of Howy and Glen. "We're concerned about the two women and dog." He placed a business card on the counter. "If you see them again, please call night or day."

Jenny had her fingers over her lips, then removed them and picked up the card. "I think you need to hear the rest of the story."

CHAPTER THIRTY-SEVEN

Hawkman and Harmon gave Jenny their full attention.

"You didn't tell me, but I have a feeling you're looking for them to be in a faded green 1973 Chevy pickup, registered to an Ed Bassett, supposedly Howy's uncle. I'm expecting him to pick it up any day."

The men exchanged glances. "I'm sure you're getting the picture now. The truck is stolen."

"I figured as much from what you've told me. However, I had no idea at the time I made the transaction to sell my older car to them. They paid me cash and gave me my full asking price with the understanding I'd store the truck until," she glanced down at the registration, "Mr. Bassett could pick it up."

"You've done nothing wrong," Harmon said.

"Maybe not, but I sure don't feel good about it."

"Describe the car you sold," Hawkman said.

"An older, pristine, silver colored, Cadillac Seville. It had only been driven about 75,000 miles and I'd always taken immaculate care of it."

Harmon slammed his hand on the counter top. "Damn!"

Jenny jumped at his reaction, and glanced at him with an open mouth.

"Sorry, but I think we saw that vehicle on Highway 96 as we traveled here. How long ago did they leave?"

"I really don't know. They bought the car yesterday and Howy said his friend was still feeling rotten, so he paid me for another night at the cabin. I didn't happen to see them depart, so I figure they left fairly early this morning."

Hawkman took a deep breath. "Ms Jenny, I'm sure this is going to be annoying to you, but I need to get in touch with the sheriff and have him impound Mr. Bassett's pickup. Do you by any chance remember the license plate number of the Cadillac?"

"I'm good friends with Sheriff Rayborn; I'll give him a call. I have a copy of the registration for the Cadillac. Give me a few minutes and I'll get it."

She limped to the back of the cabin and entered her personal quarters. Within a short time, she returned carrying a sheet of paper, and handed it to Hawkman.

"Here's a copy for you of the Cadillac registration. The sheriff will be here shortly."

"Before he arrives, I'd like to ask you a couple more questions," Hawkman said.

"Sure."

"Did you see any signs of women, or did your cleaning staff find anything feminine in the cabin?"

"No, I saw nothing of any women, and I doubt my cleaning staff would report any items to me, as they don't know who's stayed in the rooms."

"What about a dog, a golden colored Labrador?"

"No, sorry."

About that time the door opened; a man so tall he not only removed his hat from his short curly red hair, but also ducked before he stepped into the cabin. Dressed in a khaki uniform, a sheriff's badge pinned to his shirt and a holstered gun hung at his waist, he nodded as he moved into the room; his side kick walked in behind him.

"Good afternoon, Ms Jenny," he said.

"How are you, Sheriff?" Jenny said. "Glad you could make it over so quickly." She gestured toward Hawkman and Harmon. "I'd like you to meet Private Investigator Tom Casey and his friend, Harmon Getty."

"This is my partner, Matt Wilson," the sheriff said.

They all shook hands, then sat down on the two couches facing each other. Jenny took her stool behind the counter.

"Ms Jenny said you needed a favor."

Hawkman gave the law officer a quick run down of what had happened involving the two robbers, mother, child, and their dog. He also told him about the pickup and Cadillac. "What I need is for the law to impound the truck, dust it for fingerprints to see if the women have been in it and examine it for blood. There's also a golden colored Labrador, the pet of the young girl, and they're inseparable. From our last reports of the two robbers being sighted, the women and dog were not with them. This makes us very concerned for the women's well being."

"I seem to remember a report coming across my desk about this case," Rayborn said.

"It probably did, but the original crime was committed quite a distance from your territory."

"Ms Jenny told me, not knowing these men were criminals, she had not only rented these two a cabin, but sold her car to them."

Harmon glanced up at Jenny. "Do you have a copy machine?"

"Yes."

He then turned to Hawkman. "Let her make copies of those two clods and one of the Cad's registration for the sheriff."

"Good idea," Hawkman said, as he removed the items from his pocket, and handed them to her.

She left the room again. When she returned, she handed the copies to the sheriff.

"Put an alert out on the Cadillac when you can," Harmon said. "I'm sure we saw that vehicle going north on Highway 96. We didn't have any idea they would be in such a fancy car; we were looking for the Chevy pickup." Harmon held up his hand. "By the way, the sooner we can get the pickup back to the owner, the better; right now the old fellow has no transportation."

"We'll get right on it," Sheriff Rayborn said. He glanced at Ms Jenny. "Where is this pickup?"

She led them outside to the side yard where Hawkman and Harmon swung open the big double gate.

"Yep, that's Ed's truck," Harmon said.

The sheriff had stayed back and made a call on his cell phone. When he finished, he stepped forward and peered into the enclosure. "Just leave the gate open; I contacted a tow truck who's in the area and will be here in the next fifteen to twenty minutes. He'll take it to the Yreka police lab. I'll let Detective Chandler know it's on the way and he can oversee a complete report. Meanwhile, I'll get back to my office and get an alert sent out about these two men in the Cadillac."

Hawkman handed the sheriff one of his business cards. "Please keep me informed; that number will reach me night or day."

Rayborn took the card. "I'll surely let you know if we catch those two."

"Thanks."

Harmon turned to Ms Jenny. "Are you going to be all right?"

She smiled. "I'll be fine. Those men have no reason to come back here."

"We'll patrol her place for the next twenty-four hours to make sure they don't return."

"Thank you, sheriff. I appreciate that."

Hawkman extended his hand to Sheriff Rayborn. "Good meeting you."

They shook hands and the sheriff turned to Harmon. "Best of luck in finding the two women. We'll pray they're safe and will keep our eyes out for them also."

Harmon nodded. "We're going to head north on Highway 96. We'll also be on the lookout."

***

Annie awakened to the sounds of Babs moaning. Knowing her daughter had endured much pain, but trying to be brave, she decided she had no alternative; she had to find help.

Lucy lifted her head and perked her ears as Annie gently removed her arm from under Babs' neck. Between the weight of Babs' head and the hard ground, the limb had gone into a tingling sleep. Annie had to vigorously rub it to bring the feeling back.

The morning sun warmed her, so she sat up, pulled the hood off her head, tried to fluff the dirty hair. Soon giving up, she smoothed back the mane into a pony tail and tied it with the filthy ribbon she'd carried during this whole adventure.

She glanced at her daughter's ankle. It shocked her to see it had swollen terribly, and turned a horrible shiny purple. Babs moved, opened her eyes and let out a cry.
Lucy whined as Annie grabbed her daughter and hugged her close.

"I'm here, honey. I wish I could do something to make the pain go away."

"Mom, you've got to go get help. I can't stand this much longer."

"I hate to leave you here alone."

"Lucy will stay with me."

"Do you have water left?"

"Yes," she said, lifting the half full bottle from her waist. "But you don't have any."

"I'll be fine."

"No, wait, look in the backpack. I think I felt a bottle in the bottom compartment. Check it out."

Annie lifted the pack. "It does feel heavier than it should with just a few cans of meat left." She ran her hand around in the bottom and pulled out not one, but two small bottles of water. "Hey, we hit the jackpot. Even found one for Lucy."

Babs forced a smile. "Okay, Mom, go."

Annie kissed her daughter on the cheek, stood and started toward the highway.

CHAPTER THIRTY-EIGHT

The horrible memory of meeting up with Howy and Glen sent Annie's heart pounding in her ears and gave her stomach the jitters. They might be miles away. If only she knew for sure. Regardless, she had to get help for Babs. She continued her trek and could finally see the long snake like road winding through the countryside. At least she could tell if a pickup approached from either direction. It would give her time to find a hiding place before it got even with her.

She reached the shoulder of the highway, looked back and memorized landmarks so she'd know exactly where to go when she returned. Happy Camp seemed the best place to get help, if no one stopped on the road. She had no idea how far she'd have to travel, but she crossed the highway, and headed north.

The sunshine shot warm rays against her back. She eventually removed the hooded sweatshirt and tied it around her waist. Even though she had her thumb stuck out, cars zoomed past going sixty, seventy or even eighty miles per hour. She figured she appeared like a street urchin no one wanted to pick up on a desolate road. Her clothes and hair were filthy. She had no idea how dirty her face looked, but from observing Babs', she assumed she didn't look too clean either.

With the sun glaring off the vehicles, she couldn't tell the color, so any time one resembling a pickup came into her view, she quickly ran toward the trees and hid behind a thick trunk until it passed. She finally sat down on a fallen log, exhausted, thirsty and hungry.

Closing her eyes, she thought about Babs, praying she would be okay. Taking a few minutes, she ate the can of ground meat, drank a few gulps of water, then got on her way.

***

Early in the morning, Howy and Glen piled into their newly acquired car, and drove out of the Jenny's Cabins complex. When Howy reached the highway, he had his blinker on to turn south.

"No, turn north," Glen shouted.

Howy put on the brakes. "We've got to get out of this area or end up in jail for sure. How long do you think it will be before news of us buying Ms Jenny's Cadillac gets circulated? The cops will soon put it together and we won't be safe around here. Right now we've probably got enough hours to make it to the coastline and disappear."

"Don't worry; we can do what I want and be out of here before you know it."

"Are you still set on raping Annie?"

"Yes, I got a sweet feel of those soft boobs before that stupid daughter of hers put the knife to me. I have to teach that kid a lesson."

"Glen, you're really being outrageous. We have no idea where they are, and I don't want any part of your crazy scheme. I'd like to save my own neck and be able to spend some of this money we got from the bank."

"Dammit, just turn north and get off your lecture kick."

Howy exhaled loudly and turned north. "I don't like this one bit."

"You'll get over it."

"Answer me this; how do you plan to hold her down with just one arm? She's a gutsy gal and could knee you in the balls; or claw your eyes."

"You can hold her down for me."

Howy shot him a mean glare. "I told you; count me out. I ain't getting involved in any of it. You're on your own."

"Don't you want a piece?"

"Shut up, Glen, you're making me sick."

Glen reared back and laughed. "What are you, a pervert?"

Howy reached over and turned on the radio. It popped on a news station and before he could turn the dial, an alert announcement came on. "The sheriffs of Siskiyou, Shasta, and Trinity counties are asking the public's help to be on the lookout for a 2004 silver Cadillac Seville," and they recited the license number. The two men occupying it are considered armed and dangerous. Do not approach them; call 911 about their location."

Howy flipped off the radio, and hit his hands against the steering wheel. "That didn't take long. Glen, I'm turning around and getting out of these counties."

He glanced at Glen only to see the barrel of a gun pointed at his head.

"You'll do what I tell you to do," he said, his eyes narrowed to an evil glare.

"So you'd shoot your partner in crime?"

"Don't tempt me."

"All that fever you ran must have affected your brain, causing your sex drive to over-come your self preservation. If that's the case, you could have any hussy you wanted in any town with the money you now have."

"If I could drive, I'd kick you out and take over."

"Hey, I'll be happy to pull over anytime."

"Just keep your hands on the wheel and shut your mouth."

Howy took a deep breath, but kept driving in silence. Glen began to wiggle and squirm.

"What the hell's wrong with you," Howy asked.

"You gotta pull off at the next country road; I gotta shit. I can't wait much longer."

Howy rolled his eyes, and soon spotted a dirt path leading up into some trees. He pulled into the alcove of pines and stopped the engine. "Okay, get out and go do your job."

Glen put his gun into his pocket and put out his hand. "Give me the keys."

"Why?"

"I wouldn't put it past you to take off without me."

Howy pulled the keys from the ignition, and handed them to him. "Try not to take forever."

Glen grabbed the keys and opened the door. "Is there any napkins in this car?"

Howy glanced around and spotted a box of tissue. He pulled a batch out and handed them to him. "Hope that's enough for your big butt."

"Kiss my ass," Glen said and slammed the car door.

Howy snickered as he watched Glen walk deeper into the brush. "I'd laugh myself silly if he squatted in poison oak."

It seemed like thirty minutes had passed when Glen suddenly dashed out, hanging on to his dragging pants with his good hand. He jumped into the Cadillac, sweat on his face.

"What the hell?" Howy asked.

"A snake came crawling toward me."

"Did you finish your job?"

"You bet, I had no problem after that," he said, pulling up his jeans, buckling them and zipping up. "Let's get rolling."

***

Hawkman and Harmon jumped into the 4X4 and headed north on Highway 96.

"I don't know how we'll catch up. Those two idiots have gotten a good hour or two on us," Harmon said.

"Yeah, I know, wish I'd told Sheriff Rayborn to tell his men to ignore us if we were spotted speeding."

Harmon thumbed his fingers on the dashboard. "What I don't understand is why they're going north and not south. They're headed back the way they came."

"Beats me, it doesn't make good sense," Hawkman said, pushing the accelerator. "You'd think they'd want to get out of the area."

"Tell me, when does a criminal mind use any sort of logic or good old horse sense?"

"True. Makes it hard to figure out what they're up to."

"Head for my place and let's take Baby Jane up, or we're going to waste fruitless hours searching for those two."

"I'm with you. If we spot something before we get there, we can take it on; otherwise, I think we'll have much better luck from the air."

CHAPTER THIRTY-NINE

When Hawkman pulled up the driveway to Harmon's place, he breathed a sigh of relief for not getting a speeding ticket. Little did the men realize they'd passed both Annie, hidden behind a tree, and the Cadillac with Howy and Glen, parked behind a group of trees for a potty stop.

Harmon and Hawkman scurried around the side of the house to the helicopter. The bloodhounds howled at the intruders, but Harmon yelled at them and they settled down.

"I'd better fuel up," Harmon said, pulling the gas hose around to the tank.

It took several minutes for the refueling, but soon they were lifting above the house and moving toward Highway 96. They still had a few hours left of daylight.

"We keep backtracking over territory we've covered. I can't figure out why we haven't seen any signs of Anne and Babs or the two jerks," Hawkman said, speaking through the small microphone on his head gear.

"They're there; we're just missing them. I feel it in my gut."

Hawkman smiled to himself, hearing the same terminology he'd used. "I agree. I have a feeling Howy and Glen are looking for the girls, since they headed north, but haven't connected with them yet."

"Annie and Babs will keep a lookout for the old green pickup. They won't expect them in a big Cadillac, which might prove to be dangerous, unless the girls have already found a ride."

"Well, so far, we haven't heard from any authorities, so they obviously haven't located any of them," Hawkman said.

They were soon flying above the highway.

"I'm going to swing back and forth to each side in case the girls are hiking away from the main road so they won't be seen. Can you watch both sides?"

"Yeah, I think so," Hawkman said. "You just make sure you don't run into the bulging rock sides."

***

Once Glen got situated in the car after his run in with the snake, Howy pulled back onto the road. Glen's restlessness began to nag at Howy, as he opened the glove compartment and began ruffling through the papers.

"What the hell are you looking for?" Howy asked.

"Nothing in particular. I'm bored," Glen said. "Ah, ha," he remarked, as he dragged out a pair of small binoculars. "These will help."

Glen put the glasses to his eyes and studied the roadside. "These are powerful to be so little."

Howy glanced at him. "They look like something a person might take to the opera, or a horse race."

"You think Ms Jenny was a horse race fan?"

"I see her as more of an opera admirer."

Glen shrugged his shoulders, and groaned. "Shouldn't have done that, I'm still mighty sore." He put the binoculars to his face and looked out the windshield. He immediately scooted forward in his seat. "Slow down. In fact, pull over and stop."

"What the hell for?"

Glen handed him the glasses. "Look up ahead. What do you see?"

"I see a woman running toward a car that's stopped on the shoulder. My God, it looks like Annie."

"Exactly my thought. Let's just stay here a moment and see what happens. I don't see her kid anywhere."

Howy swung the optical instrument around to take in the immediate area. "I don't see her or the dog either. Wonder where they are?"

Glen slapped his thigh with his good hand. "Dang it, if we'd been just a few minutes earlier we could have had her in this car."

Howy shook his head. "She wouldn't have gotten in here with us."

"She wouldn't have known we'd switched vehicles and is keeping an eye out for the rattle trap of a truck. By the time she discovered who we were, I could have snatched her.

"Yeah, that's right," Howy said. "Uh, oh, they're making a U-turn, and heading in this direction."

"Duck down and act like you're looking for something on the floorboard."

Both men lowered their heads as the car passed.

Glen straightened in the seat, and pointed. "Follow them."

Howy decided against arguing with him, as he'd rather travel south than head back into the area where they'd committed the bank robbery. The police were alerted of their being in the Cadillac, so it really didn't matter which direction they went. He had the feeling their running from the law would soon end. Checking both directions, Howy pulled onto the highway and headed south.

"Don't get too close, I don't want them suspicious that we're following; and I sure don't want Annie looking around, as she'd for sure recognize us."

Howy frowned. "Obviously, Annie, being on the right side of the highway, wanted to go north. It puzzles me why they turned around and are now headed south."

"Beats me," Glen said. "Who cares. At least I have her in my sight and just knowing it gets me aroused."

"Good grief, you sound like a sex fiend."

Glen bounced his feet up and down on the floorboard. "It's been a long time and just thinking about touching the woman makes me horny."

Howy glanced into the rearview mirror. "I think we better pull off and get this car hidden under some trees."

"How come?"

"There's a helicopter flying this way, and going from side to side; like it's looking for something. It could be a police copter."

Glen turned in the seat and saw the speck in the sky. "You're right. Find a place to hide and we can catch up to the Ford when it passes."

Howy spun the car onto what appeared to be a country road and hit the accelerator. He made another turn on a dirt path which put them behind a hill from the road. He made a U-turn and pulled to a stop near the mound. "This should keep us out of sight, yet I can still see when the aircraft flies past."

They both stared intently at the gap in the hills.

Glen pointed. "There it goes. Ease on up to the highway."

Howy started the engine and drove up to the main road. "I think we're far enough behind the copter."

Glen put the binoculars up to his face. "I don't see any indication of it being a police craft. Wonder who they are?"

"Maybe a rancher looking for some lost cows."

"Very probable."

"Looks like it's gone ahead of the Ford."

"Good. Keep the car in sight."

***

Hawkman, studying the landscape, suddenly jerked his head back to an area he'd just scanned. "I think I just saw a dog that resembled Lucy running up to a spot that looks like an indentation or a cave." He pointed. "Would it be too dangerous to swing toward that area?"

Harmon glanced toward the hills. "Can't get real close, but maybe you can spot any activity with the binoculars."

Hawkman adjusted the glasses as Harmon turned the helicopter. When he got as close as he dared, he hovered for several minutes, watching all around. "There's a car coming up that dirt road."

CHAPTER FORTY

Sweat ran down Annie's back and her stomach growled as she hadn't eaten anything for several hours. She'd left the last cans of meat for Babs and Lucy. She'd just about given up on anyone picking her up, when a man and woman in a new black Ford Focus pulled to the shoulder in front of her.

She raced to the passenger side as the young woman rolled down the window. "Can you give me a ride to Happy Camp. My daughter is up in the hills with a broken ankle, and I need to get help."

"Sure," the young man said. "Climb in."

Annie hopped into the back seat. "Thank you so much. My name is Annie Jones."

"Hi, Annie, I'm Carl and this is my new wife, Carolyn. We're on our honeymoon."

"Congratulations."

"So how come you're out here in no man's land with no wheels?" Carl asked.

"It's a long story, but my daughter fell while we were hiking and broke her ankle. She's in a lot of pain and I hated to leave her, but I had to, as no one would find us up in those hills. Her dog won't desert her, and will protect her to a point."

"Could we reach her in this car?"

"I think so."

"It would probably be faster to try before driving all the way into Happy Camp, then back again."

"It's up to you. This is a beautiful vehicle and I sure wouldn't want anything to happen to it."

Carl glanced back at Annie. "If it can't take a rough road, then I'll take it back. I maintain my automobiles, but I'm not going to pamper them."

Annie smiled. "Thank you."

He turned around and headed south. "Let me know where to go."

Annie scooted forward in the seat so she could see better and watched for the landmarks she'd memorized. "It seems like I've walked for hours, but we're probably only about three or four miles from the turn off."

Carolyn reached down into the ice chest she had at her feet. "I bet you're hungry. How about a turkey sandwich?"

"Do you have plenty?" Annie asked.

"Yes. Here's a soda also."

Not realizing how hungry she was, Annie devoured the food. "That was delicious." She looked out the window. "We're getting close. It won't look like much more than a cow path leading into the hills."

Carl pointed ahead. "Is that it?"

Annie grasped the back of the seat, and focused on the spot. "Yes."

Carl slowed and bounced over the ridge of the highway onto the dirt. "Where now?"

"Follow the trail if you can. It should take us right to the foot of the hill where Babs hurt herself."

Carolyn pointed toward the sky. "There's a helicopter. Do you think someone's looking for you?"

"I have no idea. I don't know how they'd know where to look."

Carl had to slow to almost a snail's pace as he made his way through the trees. "Sure glad this car isn't any wider; we'd never make it."

Annie bit her lip as she studied the area and spotted several of the landmarks she'd memorized, so she knew they were getting closer. She saw the crooked tree that marked the beginning of the hill and gestured. "Stop next to that funny looking tree. We'll have to hike up the small incline and carry her down. Do you have a blanket we can use as a makeshift stretcher?"

Carl parked under the tree. "Better than that, we have a light weight collapsible steel camp cot with very short legs that fold. If she isn't real heavy, two of us can carry her." He jumped out of the car and opened the trunk.

Annie spotted a blanket and held it up. "Can I take this in case she's chilling with a fever?"

"Sure."

Carolyn scooted out of the car. "I'm coming too; it may take three of us to handle the cot."

Annie led the way and when she approached Babs' hideaway, Lucy bounded out barking. "Lucy, it's okay, it's me." The dog whined and wagged her tail. Dropping to her knees, Annie touched Babs' face. "Honey, I'm back with help to get you to a hospital."

Babs groaned as her eyelids flitted open. "Mom, it hurts so bad."

"I know, honey. If you can deal with it a little while longer, we'll get you help."

Carl came in behind Annie and glanced at Babs' badly swollen ankle. "Glad I have the cot; moving that leg is going to cause more pain."

"Just get me out of here," Babs gasped. "I'll bear it."

Carl opened and locked the cot in place then stepped toward Babs. "Annie, you and Carolyn hold this as steady as you can. I'm going to lift her and place her on it."

Annie signaled for Lucy to move out of the way.

Carl gently put an arm around Babs' back, then another under her knees. "I'm going to move slowly, but when your ankle is free of the ground, it may hurt like hell. Take a hold of me and squeeze hard; I'll understand. Tell me when you're ready."

Babs wrapped her arms around Carl's neck. "Okay, I'm ready."

He lifted her slowly off the ground and noticed her eyes closed as she bit her lip, then suddenly she went limp. "She's fainted. Get the cot closer and we'll get her on it while she's unconscious."

Carl gently placed her on the canvas and carefully straightened out her leg. "Okay, let's get her to the car."

Annie placed the blanket over Babs, then grasped the foot end of the bed, while Carolyn took the head beside her husband. They concentrated on inching their way down the incline and finally reached the Ford.

***

The Ford went around a curve in the highway and disappeared from Howy's sight for a few seconds. When the Cadillac made the same turn, Glen yelled. "Where the hell did they go?"

"They couldn't have vanished into thin air," Howy said.

Glen took the binoculars and searched both sides of the road. "I don't see any sight of them parked or any signs of turnoffs."

"We weren't far behind them; they're bound to be nearby."

"Damn!" Glen screamed. "We gotta find them."

Howy shook his head and exhaled loudly. "Where do you propose to look?"

Glen was busy scanning the landscape. He suddenly pointed toward the foothills. "Does that look like a dirt cloud? Something a car would make driving over a dirt road."

Howy did a quick look as traffic would allow. "Yeah, I'd say so."

"Okay, turn around. There must be a country lane back there."

"Why in the world would they turn off and drive into a no man's land?"

"Who the hell knows; they're certainly not in front of us."

Howy turned around. "You'll have to keep a lookout; I can't do it and drive."

CHAPTER FORTY-ONE

Harmon decided to make another pass over the area where Hawkman had thought he'd seen Lucy. As they got closer, Hawkman pointed. "There're three people carrying a stretcher, slowly making it down the incline. I'm sure that's Babs on the cot like thing; it appears she's injured. Lucy is running alongside. The person carrying one end is definitely Annie. I don't recognize the other two."

"At least it isn't the two jerks," Harmon said. "I'm going to find a spot nearby where I can set Baby Jane down; we'll go in by foot and see what's happening."

Harmon swung up and circled the area. "Uh, oh. We've got problems."

Hawkman twisted his head. "Where, I don't see anything."

"You will when I move to the side."

Once the copter shifted, Hawkman looked straight down. The big silver Cadillac moved down the road kicking up a big dust cloud. "How the hell did they know about Annie being in the other car?"

"You're asking the wrong guy; but we've got to get down there pronto. Looks like the only place I'm going to be able to set down is about a block and a half away."

"Do it; the faster we get to the Ford, the better."

"I think we've got a little time, seems they're having trouble navigating through the trees with the wide Cadillac. I'd laugh if they got stuck between two big trunks."

Harmon immediately dropped the copter down and maneuvered it into a very small opening between some trees. Hawkman held his breath and gripped the door handle. When the craft landed softly, he let out a hearty exhale.

"Man, you are good."

"Thank you, kind sir."

Each man slapped on his hat, and jumped out of the air craft. Not knowing what to expect, they drew their weapons. They trotted through the underbrush toward the small hill. As they neared, they heard a scream and a shot echo through the air.

They picked up their gait and charged into a clearing where they found the Cadillac parked next to the black Ford. They came to an abrupt halt.

Glen knelt at the cot with his gun pointed at Babs' head. "Drop your guns and put your hands above your head, or else she's mincemeat."

Harmon and Hawkman dropped their weapons to the ground and raised their arms.

Howy had Annie, Carl and Carolyn at gun point. Near the tree line, Lucy barked and whined.

Annie twisted around. "No, Lucy. Stay."

Glen pointed his pistol at Annie. "Keep your mouth shut, or my next shot won't be in the air. Let the dog do what she wants."

Annie glared at him. "Why, so you can kill her?"

He grinned wickedly. "Once I get you alone, we'll see how much of a smart ass mouth you'll have." Suddenly, Glen stood and fired at the ground where Hawkman and Harmon stood. "Don't move again, or next time I won't miss."

Carl grabbed Carolyn and put her behind him.

"Those guys friends of yours?" Glen asked.

Carl shook his head. "We don't know any of you people, we're just innocent bystanders."

Glen glanced at Howy. "Isn't that the guy who fed us opossum at his place?"

"Sure looks like him."

Glen frowned. "Thought you shot him?"

"I did. He must be a tough bugger."

Glen's gaze traveled to the cot when Babs moaned and let out a cry. He moved his gun so it pointed at her head.

"No," Annie screamed, immediately dropping down and covering her daughter's body with her own.

"What's with her being on this cot? Is she sick?" Glen asked.

Annie glared up at him. "She broke her ankle while we were up in the hills trying to stay away from you two. I need to get her to a hospital."

He laughed. "Does my heart good to think she's in misery; she'll know how I've felt ever since she knifed me."

"Point your blasted gun in a different direction," Annie said, as she stood and pushed the barrel away.

"Now don't get feisty, pretty lady," Glen said, I've got plans for you very soon. "Actually, we could get in the Cad and have a little foreplay. Howy can keep his eye on this bunch."

Annie narrowed her eyes. "I wouldn't go anywhere with you, you scum ball." Then she spit on him.

Glen raised the hand with the gun and smacked Annie across the face. Even though she was able to break the blunt of the strike by throwing up her arm, she let out a scream and blood gushed from her nose.

Babs had seen and heard the whole thing. She slipped the knife out of her pocket, locked the blade, brought herself into a sitting position and aimed it at Glen's back. She'd mastered this art while learning how to whittle. The knife lodged in his right shoulder.

He bellowed, then turned the gun on Babs. A shot rang out; Glen fell to his knees and turned toward Howy with a shocked look.

"What the hell? Why'd you shoot me?"

"I told you I wouldn't have anything to do with a murder," Howy said, glaring at Glen.

Glen raised his gun and shot Howy in the chest. Howy dropped and lay lifeless where he fell.

Hawkman and Harmon were within earshot of what was going on, yet too far away to make any drastic moves without getting themselves killed or someone in the party; so they remained fairly still until the opportunity arose where they could charge in.

As soon as they heard the shots, the two men grabbed their weapons from the grass and hightailed it to the scene. Hawkman checked for a pulse in both Glen and Howy; he found none.

"We won't have to worry about those two anymore," Hawkman said, turning toward Babs.

"How are you faring?"

"Okay, as long as I don't move. Where's Lucy?"

Hawkman stared at her. "You actually spoke. When did you get your voice back?"

"When that lowlife tried to rape my Mom."

"You can tell me about that later; right now, we've got to get you and Annie to a hospital pronto." Hawkman let out a whistle. "Come, Lucy."

The dog bounded from the tree line into the knit of people, and headed straight to Babs' side. Lucy paced beside the cot whining, yet wagging her tail.

Carl and Carolyn were frozen to the spot, until Hawkman got their attention.

"Do you by any chance have an ice chest, so we can make a pack for Annie's nose?"

"Yes," Carolyn said. She pulled away from behind Carl, and opened the car door of the Ford.

Hawkman spotted Harmon outside the ring of people with his cell phone to his ear. Harmon soon walked toward Hawkman. "Got ahold of the authorities and they're on their way. I told them I'd fly Babs and Annie to the hospital."

Carl stepped up to the two men. "I don't know who you are, but assume you're the good guys."

Hawkman grinned. "Yes, you can say that. What can we do for you?"

"I'm wondering how long we'll be detained. Carolyn and I just got married and are on the first leg of our honeymoon. We'd like to get on with it."

Harmon put his hand on the young man's shoulder. "Congratulations. She's a beautiful young woman, and I wish you lots of happiness."

"Thank you."

"The sheriff will need a statement from you and where he can reach you after you return from your trip. I'll put a bug in his ear to let you kids get on your way."

"I appreciate it,"Carl said, as Carolyn walked past, carrying an ice pack to Annie.

It wasn't long before a parade of county police cars, coroner's wagon and a tow truck came barreling down the dirt road. True to his word, Harmon talked to the sheriff about Carl and Carolyn, so the officer spoke with them first, and let them leave.

The coroner did his preliminaries, then loaded Glen's and Howy's bodies into the wagon. Hawkman and Harmon made appointments to go see the sheriff at his office the next day, then they gently picked up Bab's stretcher and made their way to the helicopter; Annie followed with Lucy bringing up the rear.

Once they loaded everyone, plus Lucy, into the air craft, Harmon and Hawkman climbed into the cockpit. Harmon turned on the rotors and the copter lifted above the treetops and they were off to the Yreka hospital.

CHAPTER FORTY-TWO

Harmon set the helicopter down in the parking lot, near the emergency entrance. Hawkman jumped out and alerted the team who then loaded Babs and Annie onto two gurneys, then rolled them inside.

"Lucy, stay," Harmon said, as she was ready to go with Babs. Lucy whined, but sat down on her haunches.

"I'll get things situated and be back in a few minutes," Hawkman said, as he dashed into the hospital.

When he returned to the air craft, Harmon already had Lucy loaded, so he climbed aboard. Once settled, and Harmon lifted off, Hawkman told him what the doctor said.

"More than likely, Babs will have to go into surgery with the broken ankle. Since Annie is with her, she can sign all the papers. The doctor didn't think Annie's nose was broken, but wanted to take some x-rays."

"What's plan two?" Harmon asked.

"I'll pick up my vehicle at your place and head for Luke's, give him the news and drop off Lucy. His truck is in working order, so he can go into town and pick up the girls when the doctor releases them."

"I'm sure he'll be one relieved man to know his family is whole, and the criminals will never bother them again."

Hawkman nodded. "Thanks to you and Baby Jane; without you it could never have been accomplished."

Harmon grinned. "All in the line of duty."

***

Hawkman left Harmon's place with Lucy and headed for the Jones' home. When he pulled up in front, he let Lucy out and she dashed to the front door where Luke stood.
He eyed Hawkman with skepticism as he approached.

"Where are my girls?" he asked, his lips quivering.

"Both your women are at the Yreka hospital waiting for you. Babs has a badly broken ankle and will probably need surgery. Annie has a terribly bruised face and will look like she's been through a war zone, but they're alive and will be good as new in no time. They can tell you the whole story much better than I can. Oh, and I might add, those two robbers will never bother anyone again."

Tears welled in Luke's eyes. "Thank the Lord above. I'm getting my coat and heading to the hospital."

Hawkman handed Luke a hundred dollar bill. "Babs may not be released tonight, so get a motel room for you and Annie, then bring Babs home tomorrow."

"Mr. Casey, I can't take your money."

"Yes, you can. I want this whole mess to end right. Having you and your family reunited will make it all come true."

Luke pulled a handkerchief from his pocket and wiped his wet cheeks.

"Why don't I take Lucy home with me," Hawkman offered. "You don't need to worry about her too. I'll check with you in a couple of days and bring her when Babs gets home."

"Are you sure you want to mess with a dog after all you've been through?" he asked, slipping on his jacket and grabbing his cane.

"Lucy is no problem. My wife loves her."

Hawkman watched Luke limp to his pickup, parked in the shed behind the house, then he called Lucy. She jumped into the passenger seat of the 4x4 without hesitation.

When Hawkman pulled into his own garage, Jennifer opened the front door. Lucy jumped out of the SUV and ran to her. As Jennifer hugged the dog, she looked up at her husband with the crease between her eyes furrowed into a deep line.

Hawkman knew she feared the worst. "Do you mind taking care of Lucy while Babs and Annie recover in the hospital?"

A big smile covered her face as she hugged her husband. "They're okay?"

"Yes," he said, putting his arm around her shoulder as they walked into the house.

Lucy immediately ran to the bedroom where she and Babs had slept, grabbed the rug Jennifer had put down for her to sleep on, dragged it into the living room and placed it right below Miss Marple's favorite spot on the hearth. The cat bowed her back and gave a hiss or two, but settled on her own spot with a defiant look at the dog.

Hawkman and Jennifer laughed, "I'm going to fix us a tall drink," she said, giving her husband a big kiss. "Then I want to hear the whole story."

THE END

ABOUT THE AUTHOR

Born and raised in Oklahoma, Betty Sullivan La Pierre attended the Oklahoma College for Women and the University of Oklahoma, graduating with her BS degree in Speech Therapy with a Specialty in the Deaf.

Once married, she moved to California with her husband. When her husband was killed in an automobile accident, she was left with two young boys to raise. She is now remarried and has had another son through that marriage.

Ms. La Pierre has lived in the Silicon Valley (California) for many years. At one time, she owned a Mail Order Used Book business dealing mainly in signed and rare books, but phased it out because it took up too much of her writing time. She's an avid reader, belongs to the Wednesday Writers' Society, and periodically attends functions of other writing organizations.

She writes Mystery/Suspense/Thriller novels, which are published in digital format and print. Her Hawkman Mystery Series is developing quite a fan base. Most of the stories are set around Copco Lake in Northern California where Hawkman lives with his wife, Jennifer. If you read the "THE ENEMY STALKS" you'll get the feel for Hawkman and where he comes from. After that, the books can be read in any order, as each is a complete story. Betty's also written two stand-alone Mystery/ Thrillers, "MURDER.COM" and "THE DEADLY THORN". She plans to continue writing until her fingers give out on the keyboard.

Betty Sullivan La Pierre's work is a testament to how much she enjoys the challenge of plotting an exciting story.
Visit her personal site at: http://bettysullivanlapierre.com